Disney **FAIRIES**

Tinker Bell

and the

LEGEND OF THE
NEVERBEAST

PAPERCUTZ™

Graphic Novels Available from
PAPERCUTZ

Graphic Novel #1
"Prilla's Talent"

Graphic Novel #2
"Tinker Bell and the
Wings of Rani"

Graphic Novel #3
"Tinker Bell and the
Day of the Dragon"

Graphic Novel #4
"Tinker Bell
to the Rescue"

Graphic Novel #5
"Tinker Bell and the
Pirate Adventure"

Graphic Novel #6
"A Present
for Tinker Bell"

Graphic Novel #7
"Tinker Bell the
Perfect Fairy"

Graphic Novel #8
"Tinker Bell and her
Stories for a Rainy Day"

Graphic Novel #9
"Tinker Bell and
her Magical Arrival"

Graphic Novel #10
"Tinker Bell and
the Lucky Rainbow"

Graphic Novel #11
"Tinker Bell and the
Most Precious Gift"

Graphic Novel #12
"Tinker Bell and the
Lost Treasure"

Graphic Novel #13
"Tinker Bell and the
Pixie Hollow Games"

Graphic Novel #14
"Tinker Bell and
Blaze"

**Tinker Bell
and the Great
Fairy Rescue**

Graphic Novel #15
"Tinker Bell and the
Secret of the Wings"

Graphic Novel #16
"Tinker Bell and the
Pirate Fairy"

Graphic Novel #17
"Tinker Bell and the
Legend of the NeverBeast"

DISNEY FAIRIES graphic novels are available in paperback for $7.99 each;
in hardcover for $12.99 each except #5, $6.99PB, $10.99HC. #6-14 are $7.99PB $11.99HC. #15 – 17 are $7.99PB $12.99HC.
Tinker Bell and the Great Fairy Rescue is $9.99 in hardcover only.
Available at booksellers everywhere.

See more at papercutz.com

Or you can order from us: Please add $4.00 for postage and handling for first book, and add $1.00 for each additional book.
Please make check payable to NBM Publishing. Send to: Papercutz, 160 Broadway, Suite 700, East Wing, New York, NY 10038
or call 800 886 1223 (9-6 EST M-F) MC-Visa-Amex accepted.

#17 "Tinker Bell and the Legend of the NeverBeast"

Contents

Heart or Head   7

Welcome, Gruff!   20

All Together Now   33

The Green Storm   46

PAPERCUTZ™

NEW YORK

Look high in the sky on this Never Land night
For a glowing green star, the fourth from the right.
As it falls from the heavens and streaks through the air.
You'll know it's a comet, a sight strange and rare.
A harmless display? A treat for the eye?

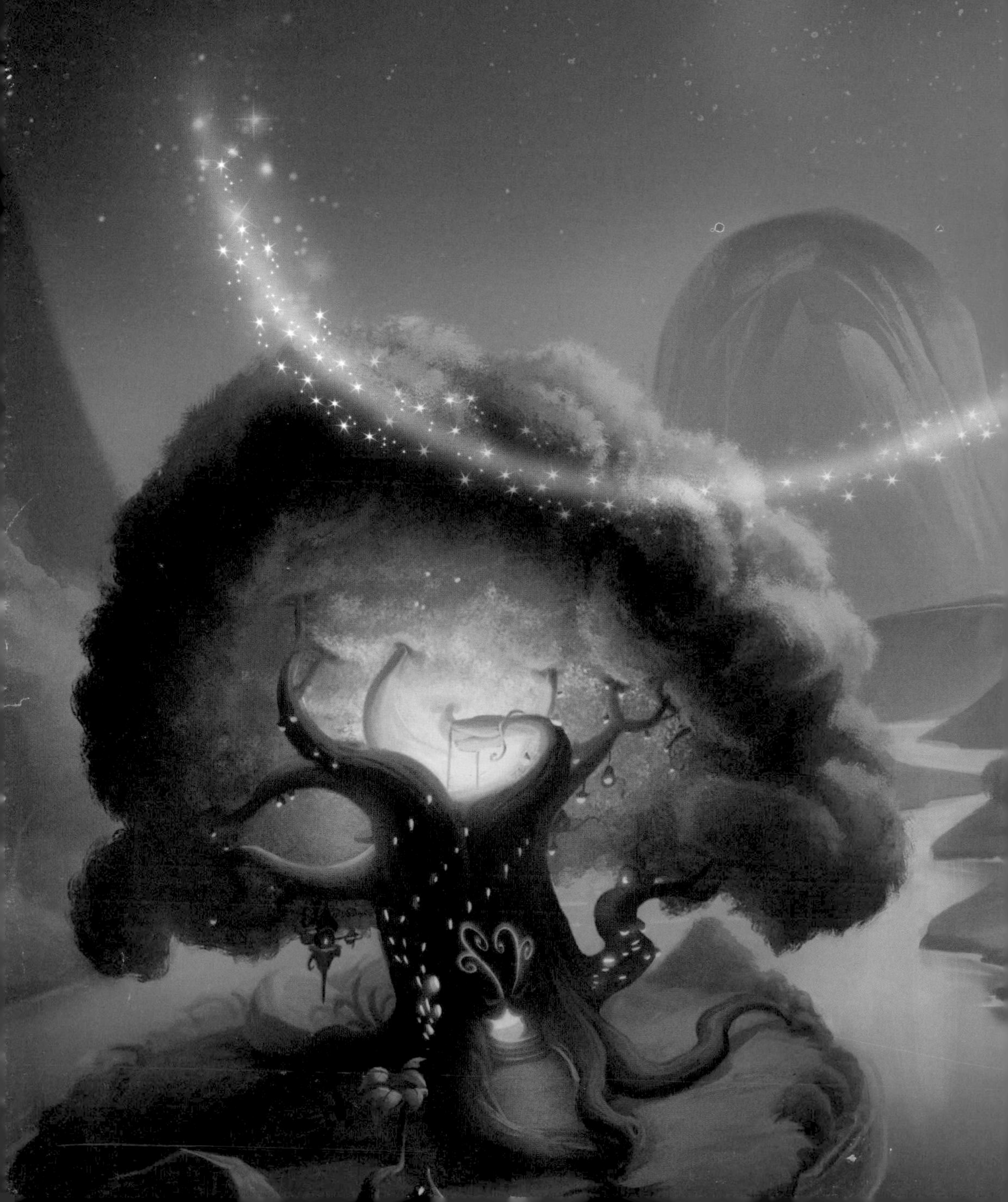

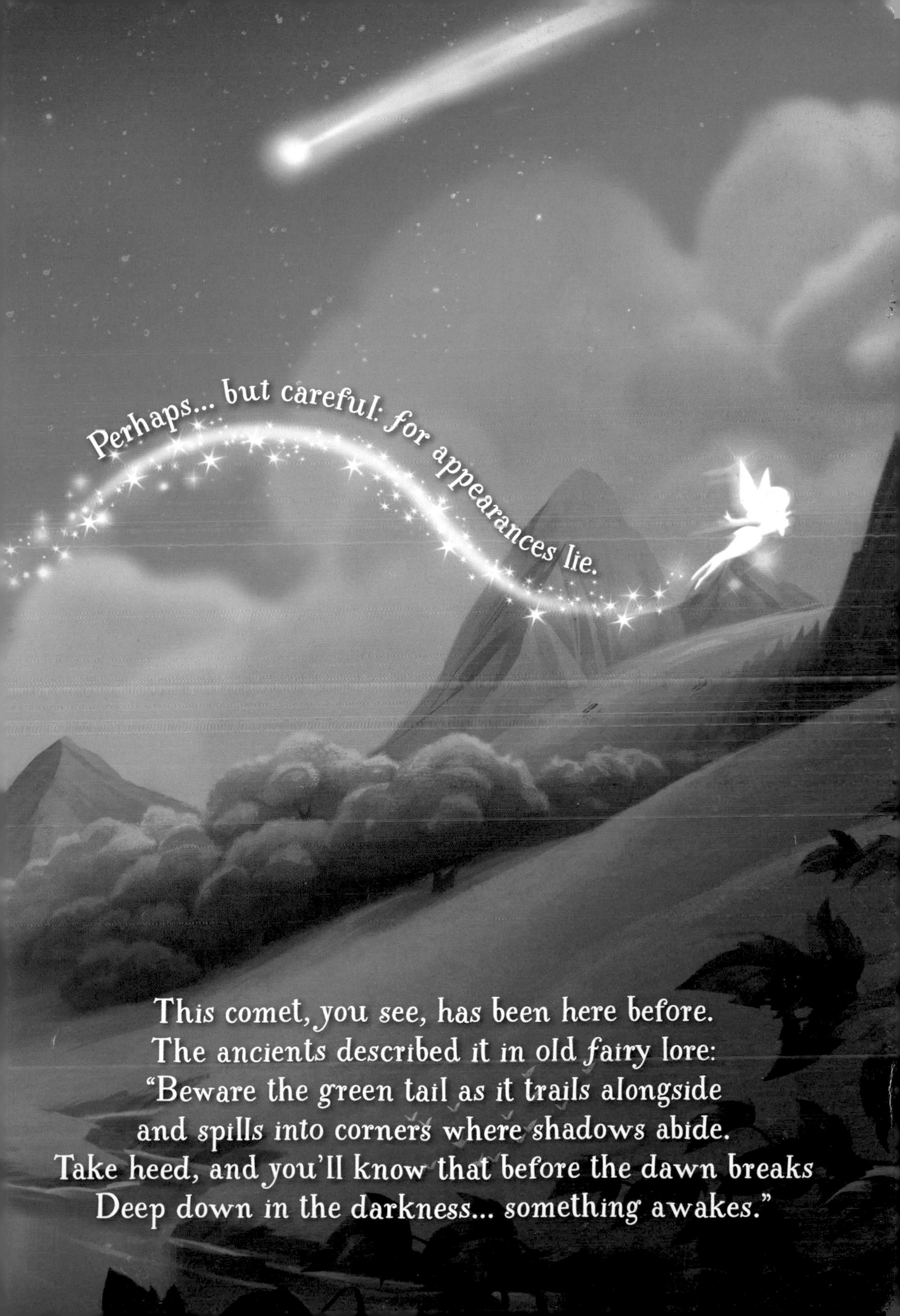

Perhaps... but careful: for appearances lie.

This comet, you see, has been here before.
The ancients described it in old fairy lore:
"Beware the green tail as it trails alongside
and spills into corners where shadows abide.
Take heed, and you'll know that before the dawn breaks
Deep down in the darkness... something awakes."

Discover fairy games and activities
at www.disneyfairies.com

is available on

"Tinker Bell and the Legend of the NeverBeast"

Script: Tea Orsi
(Based on the story by Steve Loter and Tom Rogers and the screenplay
by Tom Rogers, Robert Schooley, Mark McCorkle, and Kate Kondell.)
Revised Captions: Cortney Faye Powell and Jim Salicrup
Layout: Rosa La Barbera, Sara Storino
Clean Up: Leticia Algeri, Veronica di Lorenzo
Ink: Christina Stella, Santa Zangari
Paint: Kawaii Creative Studio
Additional Art: Denise Shimabukuro, Andrea Cagol
Special Thanks to: Heather Knowles, Vicki Letizia, Steve Loter, Ellen
Jin Over, Estefania Perez Sahonero, Kristin Peters, Makul Wigert

DISNEY PUBLISHING WORLDWIDE
Global Magazines, Comics and Partworks

Vice President, Global Magazines and New IP: Gianfranco Cordara
Editorial Director: Guido Frazzini (Director Comics)
Editorial Team: Bianca Coletti (Director, Magazines),
Stefano Ambrosio (Executive Editor, New IP),
Carlotta Quattrocolo (Executive Editor, Franchise),
Behnoosh Khalili (Senior Editor), Julie Dorris (Senior Editor)

Design: Enrico Soave (Senior Designer)

Art: Ken Shue (VP, Global Art),
Roberto Santillo (Creative Director),
Marco Ghiglione (Creative Manager),
Steffano Attardi (Computer Art Designer)

Portfolio Management: Olivia Ciancarelli (Director)

Business & Marketing: Camilla Vedove (Managing Editor),
Mariantonietta Galla (Marketing Manager),
Virpi Korhonen (Editorial Manager),
Kristen Ginter (Publishing Coordinator)

Contributors: Megan Adams, Manny Mederos, Carlo Resca

Editing – Graphic Design: Lito Milano S.r.l.,
Co-d S.r.l. – Milano

Production – Dawn K. Guzzo
Production Coordinator – Jeff Whitman
Associate Editor – Bethany Bryan
Editor-in-Chief – Jim Salicrup

ISBN: 978-1-62991-189-2 paperback edition
ISBN: 978-1-62991-190-8 hardcover edition

Printed in China
Printed July 2015 by Samfine Printing (Shenzhen) Co. Ltd
Samfine Industrial Park, Heng Hexing Industrial Zone,
Liaokeng New Villiage Shiyan Town,
Bao'an District Shenzhen, Guangdong
China

Papercutz books may be purchased for business or
promotional use. For information on bulk purchases
please contact Macmillan Corporate and
Premium Sales Department at (800) 221-7945 x5442.

Distributed by Macmillan
First Papercutz Printing

PART ONE:

"Heart or Head"

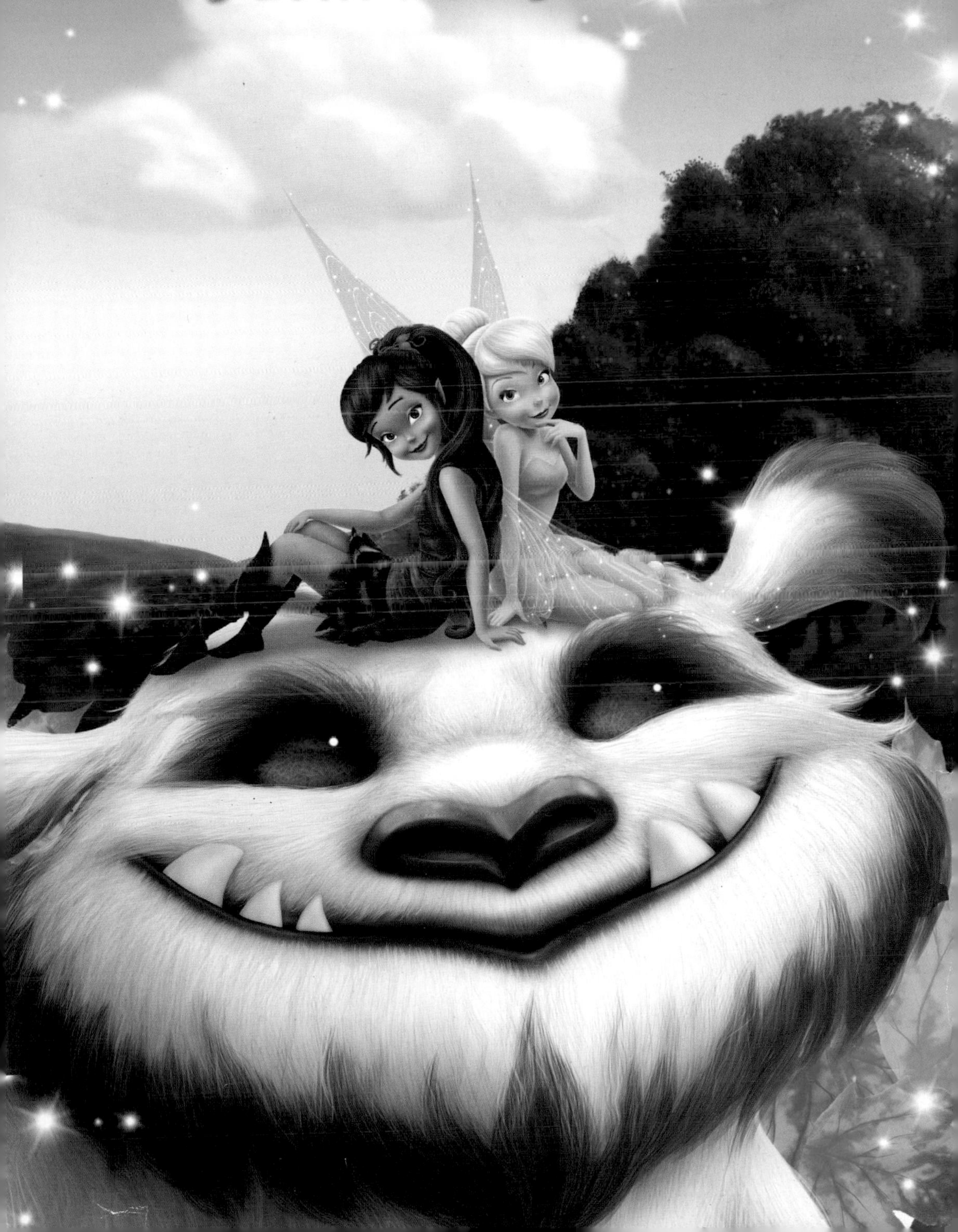

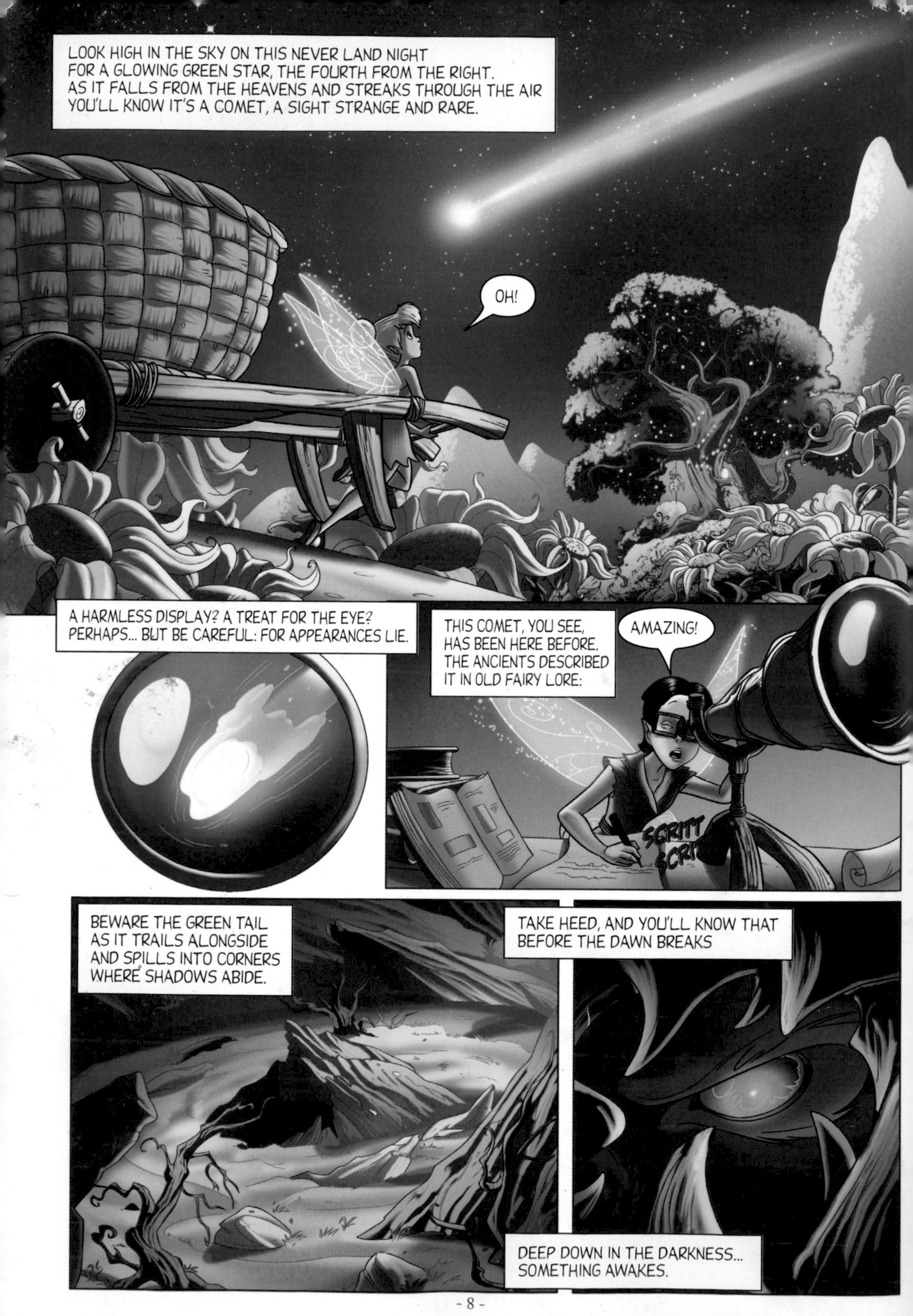
LOOK HIGH IN THE SKY ON THIS NEVER LAND NIGHT
FOR A GLOWING GREEN STAR, THE FOURTH FROM THE RIGHT.
AS IT FALLS FROM THE HEAVENS AND STREAKS THROUGH THE AIR
YOU'LL KNOW IT'S A COMET, A SIGHT STRANGE AND RARE.
OH!
A HARMLESS DISPLAY? A TREAT FOR THE EYE?
PERHAPS... BUT BE CAREFUL: FOR APPEARANCES LIE.
THIS COMET, YOU SEE, HAS BEEN HERE BEFORE. THE ANCIENTS DESCRIBED IT IN OLD FAIRY LORE:
AMAZING!
SCRITT SCRITT
BEWARE THE GREEN TAIL AS IT TRAILS ALONGSIDE AND SPILLS INTO CORNERS WHERE SHADOWS ABIDE.
TAKE HEED, AND YOU'LL KNOW THAT BEFORE THE DAWN BREAKS
DEEP DOWN IN THE DARKNESS... SOMETHING AWAKES.

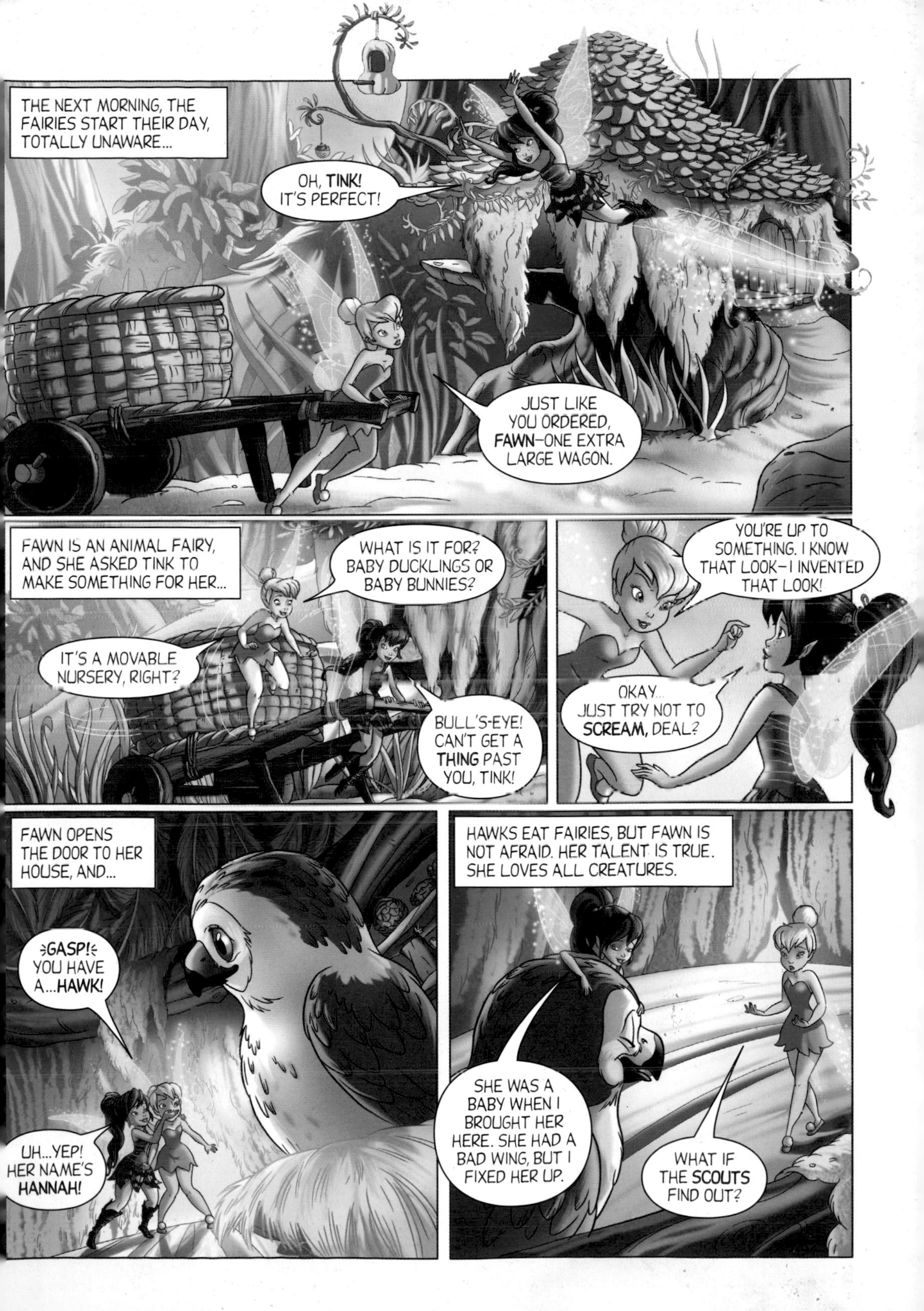

THE NEXT MORNING, THE FAIRIES START THEIR DAY, TOTALLY UNAWARE...
OH, **TINK!** IT'S PERFECT!
JUST LIKE YOU ORDERED, **FAWN**—ONE EXTRA LARGE WAGON.
FAWN IS AN ANIMAL FAIRY, AND SHE ASKED TINK TO MAKE SOMETHING FOR HER...
WHAT IS IT FOR? BABY DUCKLINGS OR BABY BUNNIES?
IT'S A MOVABLE NURSERY, RIGHT?
BULL'S-EYE! CAN'T GET A **THING** PAST YOU, TINK!
YOU'RE UP TO SOMETHING. I KNOW THAT LOOK—I INVENTED THAT LOOK!
OKAY... JUST TRY NOT TO **SCREAM,** DEAL?
FAWN OPENS THE DOOR TO HER HOUSE, AND...
GASP! YOU HAVE A...**HAWK!**
UH...YEP! HER NAME'S **HANNAH!**
HAWKS EAT FAIRIES, BUT FAWN IS NOT AFRAID. HER TALENT IS TRUE. SHE LOVES ALL CREATURES.
SHE WAS A BABY WHEN I BROUGHT HER HERE. SHE HAD A BAD WING, BUT I FIXED HER UP.
WHAT IF THE **SCOUTS** FIND OUT?

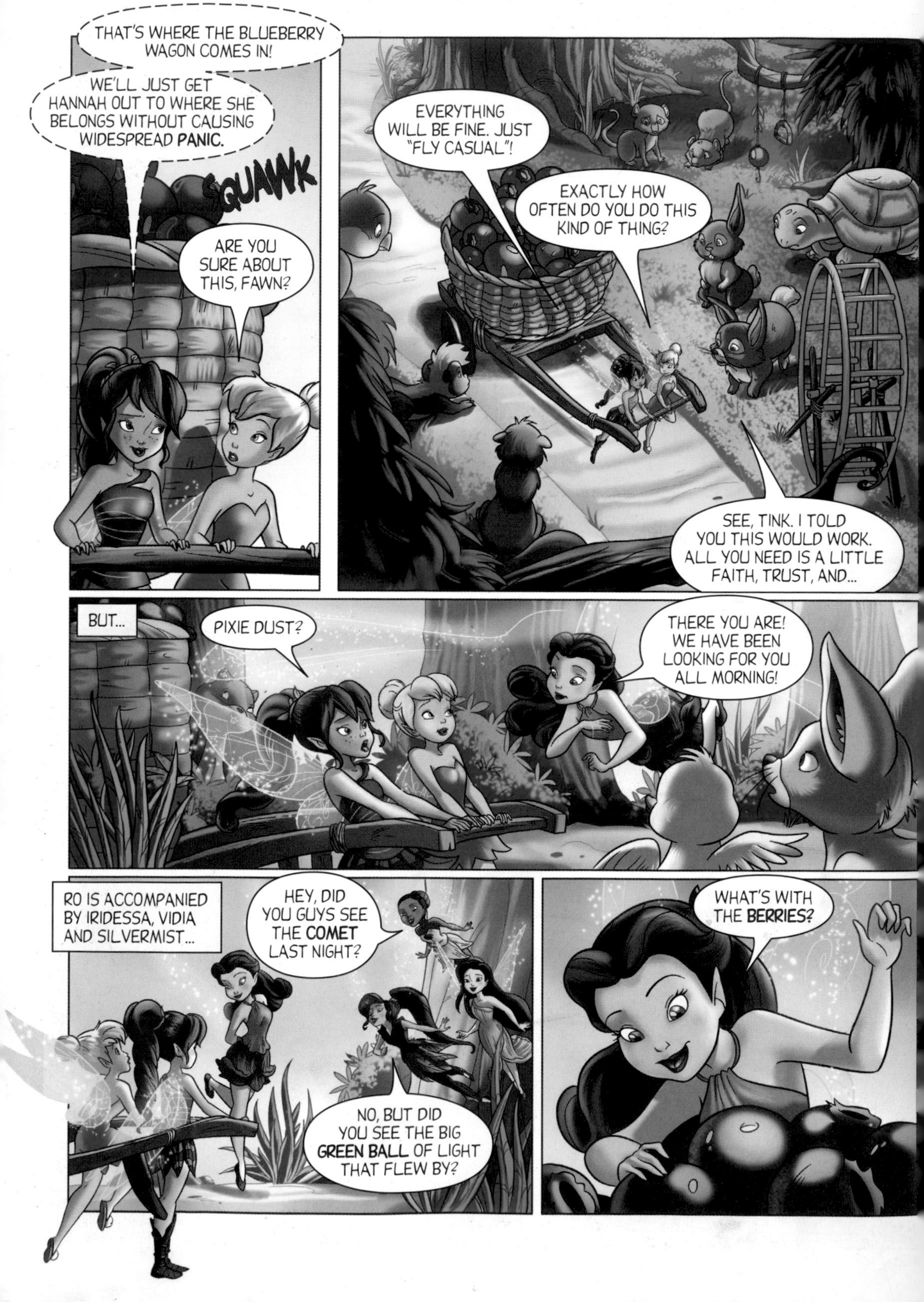

THAT'S WHERE THE BLUEBERRY WAGON COMES IN!
WE'LL JUST GET HANNAH OUT TO WHERE SHE BELONGS WITHOUT CAUSING WIDESPREAD PANIC.
SQUAWK
ARE YOU SURE ABOUT THIS, FAWN?
EVERYTHING WILL BE FINE. JUST "FLY CASUAL"!
EXACTLY HOW OFTEN DO YOU DO THIS KIND OF THING?
SEE, TINK. I TOLD YOU THIS WOULD WORK. ALL YOU NEED IS A LITTLE FAITH, TRUST, AND...
BUT...
PIXIE DUST?
THERE YOU ARE! WE HAVE BEEN LOOKING FOR YOU ALL MORNING!
RO IS ACCOMPANIED BY IRIDESSA, VIDIA AND SILVERMIST...
HEY, DID YOU GUYS SEE THE COMET LAST NIGHT?
NO, BUT DID YOU SEE THE BIG GREEN BALL OF LIGHT THAT FLEW BY?
WHAT'S WITH THE BERRIES?

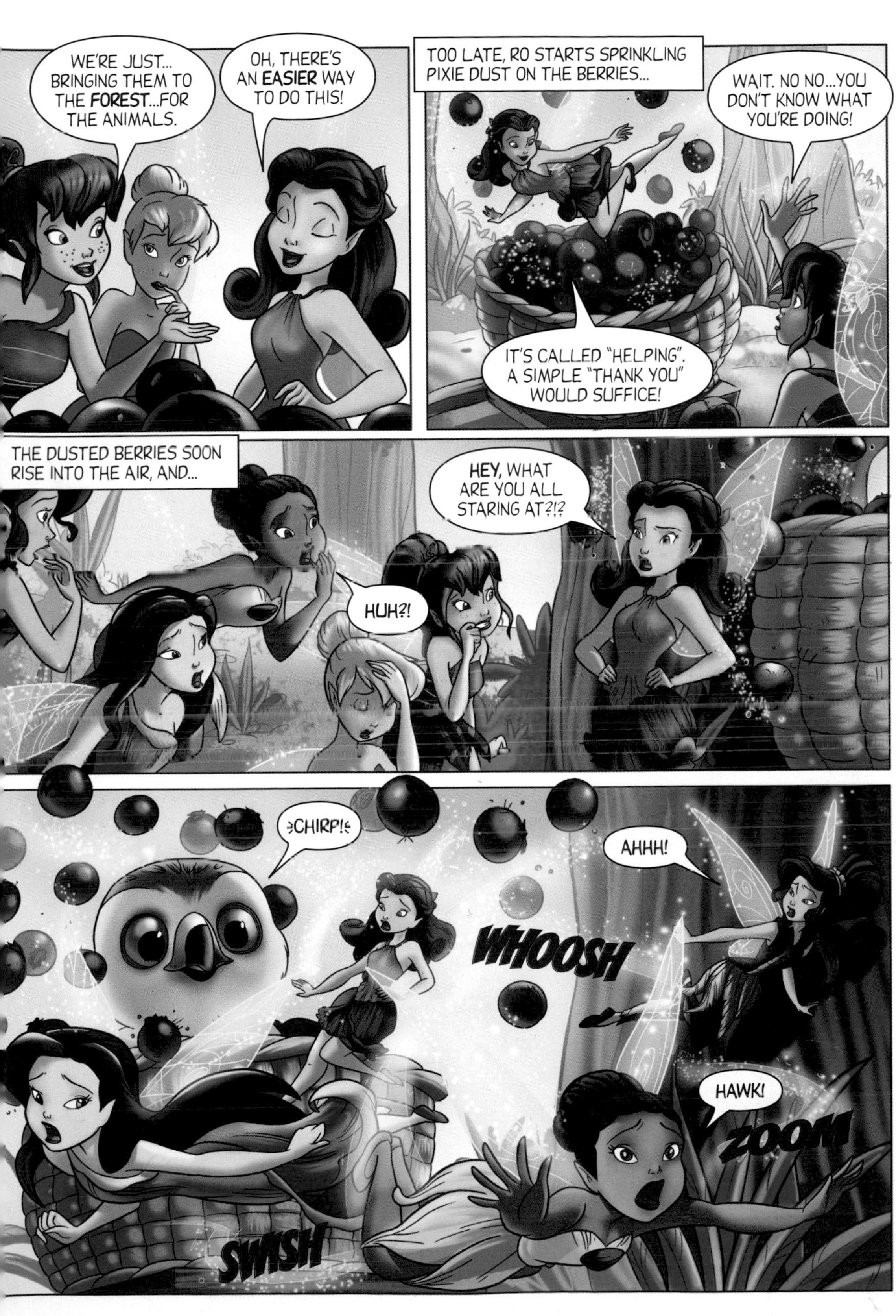
WE'RE JUST... BRINGING THEM TO THE FOREST...FOR THE ANIMALS.
OH, THERE'S AN EASIER WAY TO DO THIS!
TOO LATE, RO STARTS SPRINKLING PIXIE DUST ON THE BERRIES...
WAIT. NO NO...YOU DON'T KNOW WHAT YOU'RE DOING!
IT'S CALLED "HELPING". A SIMPLE "THANK YOU" WOULD SUFFICE!
THE DUSTED BERRIES SOON RISE INTO THE AIR, AND...
HEY, WHAT ARE YOU ALL STARING AT?!?
HUH?!
CHIRP!
AHHH!
WHOOSH
HAWK!
ZOOM
SWISH

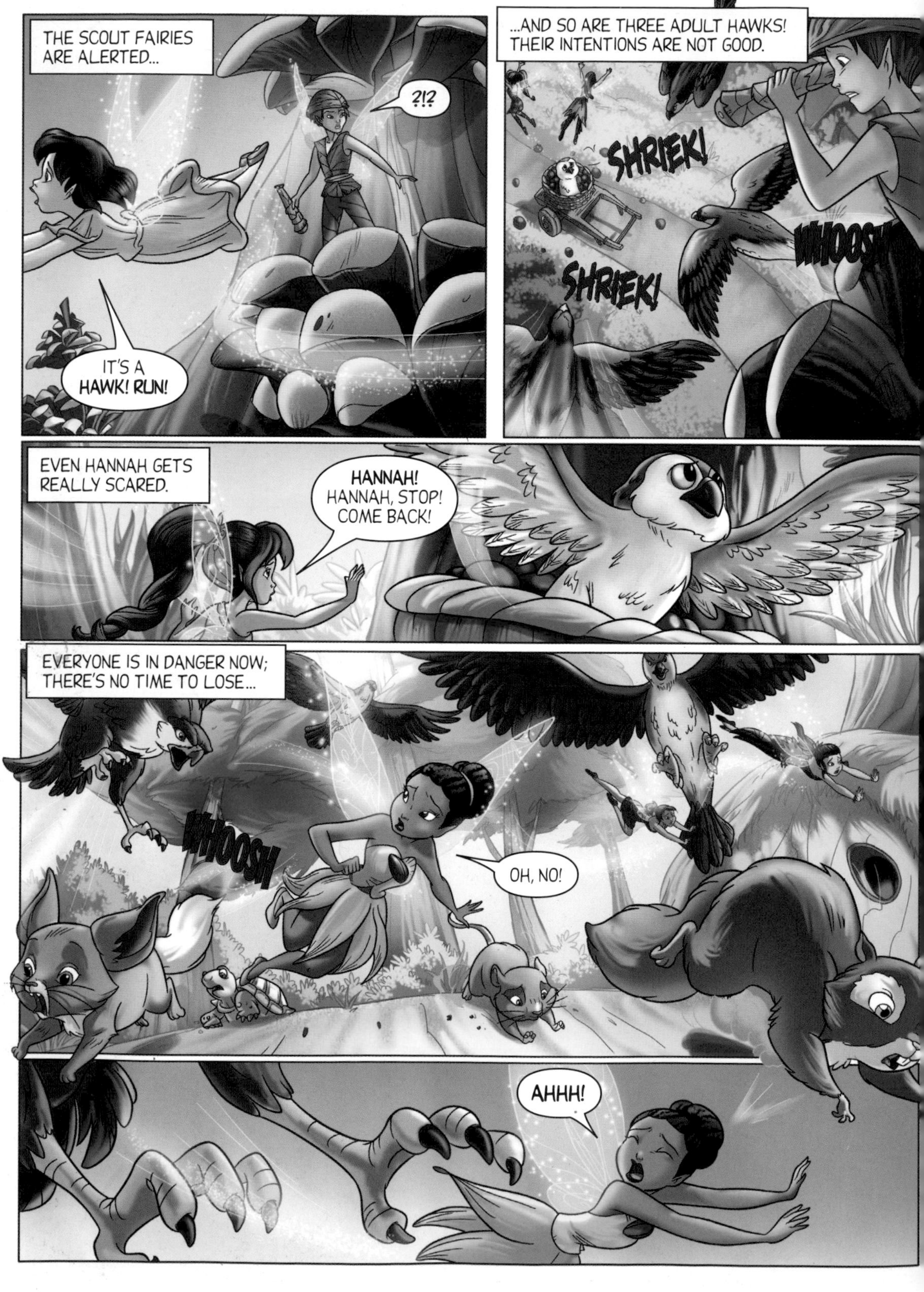
THE SCOUT FAIRIES ARE ALERTED...
?!?
IT'S A HAWK! RUN!
...AND SO ARE THREE ADULT HAWKS! THEIR INTENTIONS ARE NOT GOOD.
SHRIEK!
SHRIEK!
WHOOSH
EVEN HANNAH GETS REALLY SCARED.
HANNAH! HANNAH, STOP! COME BACK!
EVERYONE IS IN DANGER NOW; THERE'S NO TIME TO LOSE...
WHOOSH
OH, NO!
AHHH!

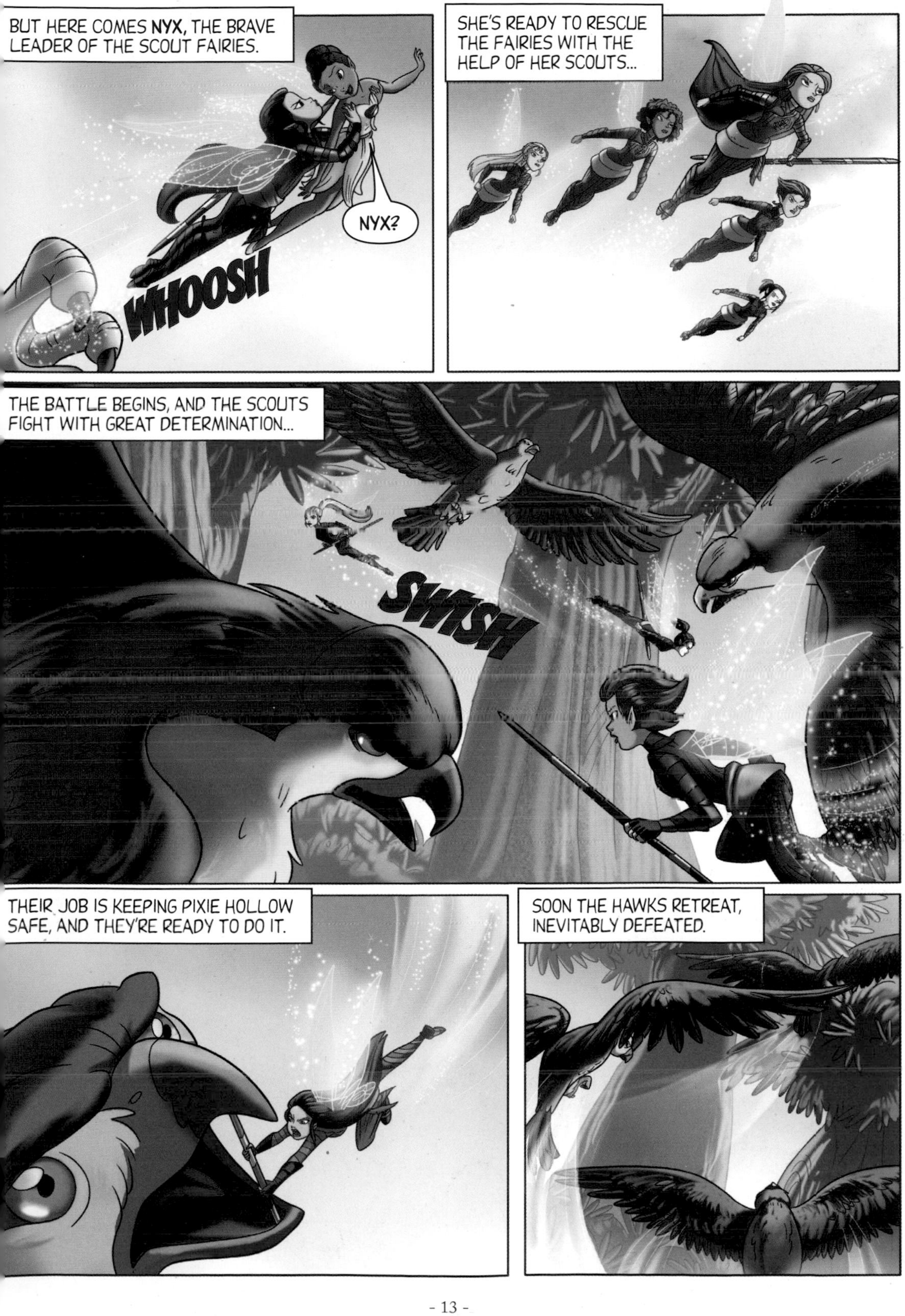
BUT HERE COMES NYX, THE BRAVE LEADER OF THE SCOUT FAIRIES.
NYX?
WHOOSH
SHE'S READY TO RESCUE THE FAIRIES WITH THE HELP OF HER SCOUTS...
THE BATTLE BEGINS, AND THE SCOUTS FIGHT WITH GREAT DETERMINATION...
SWISH
THEIR JOB IS KEEPING PIXIE HOLLOW SAFE, AND THEY'RE READY TO DO IT.
SOON THE HAWKS RETREAT, INEVITABLY DEFEATED.

BUT HANNAH'S STILL THERE, AND...

SWOSH

SHRIEK!

EVERYBODY **CALM DOWN!** I PROMISE SHE DOESN'T EVEN LIKE THE TASTE OF SCOUT FAIRIES!

GET AWAY FROM THE HAWK, FAWN. LET **US** HANDLE THIS.

THERE'S NOTHING TO HANDLE, NYX!

JUST THEN, QUEEN CLARION ARRIVES...

IS EVERYONE ALL RIGHT?

YES, BUT HOW AM I SUPPOSED TO KEEP US SAFE IF FAWN KEEPS BRINGING DANGEROUS ANIMALS INTO PIXIE HOLLOW?!

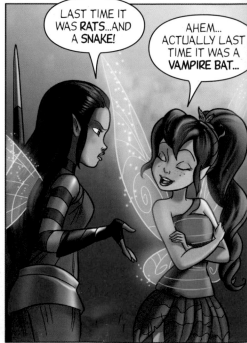

LAST TIME IT WAS **RATS**...AND A **SNAKE!**

AHEM... ACTUALLY LAST TIME IT WAS A **VAMPIRE BAT**...

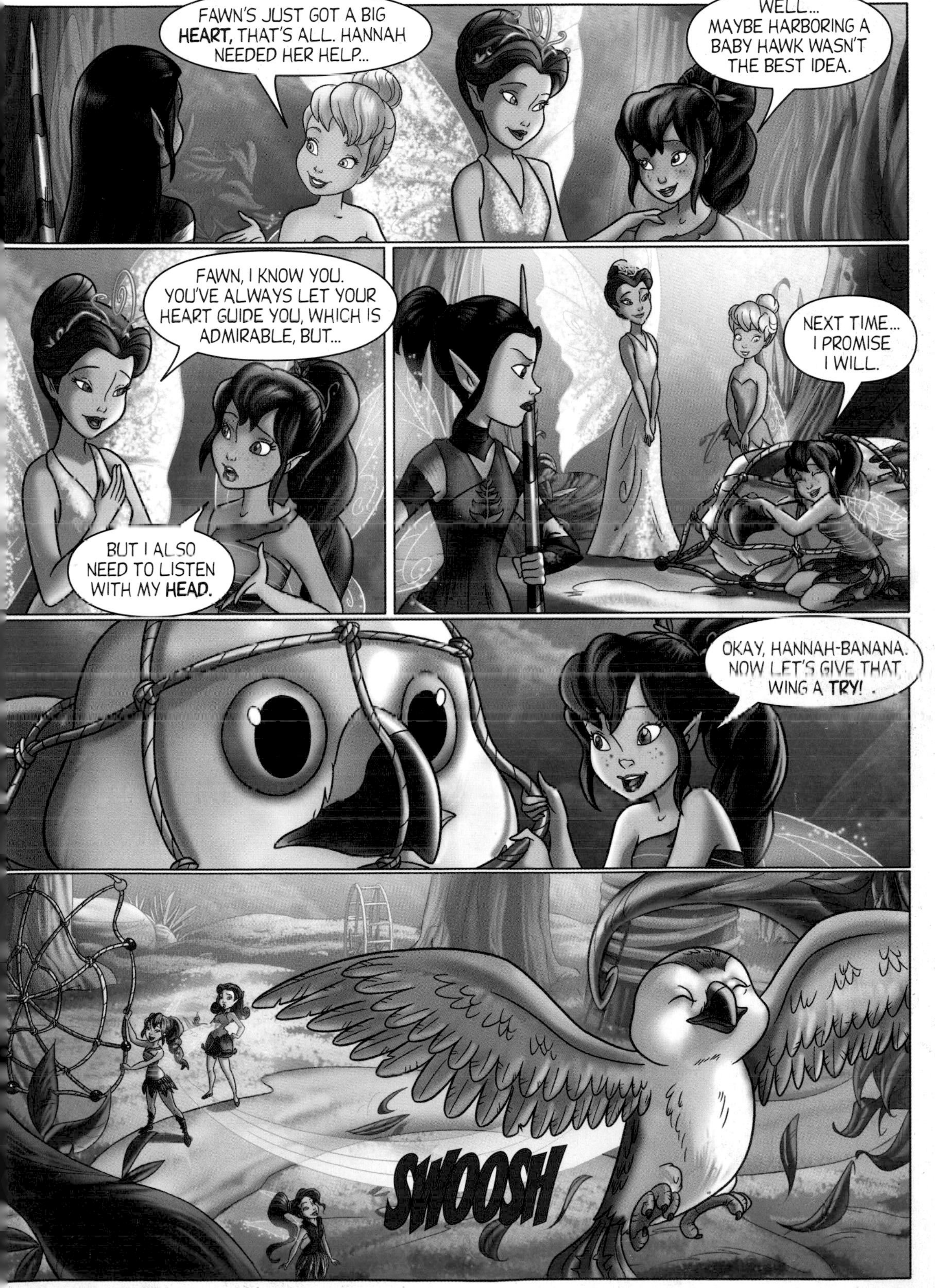
FAWN'S JUST GOT A BIG HEART, THAT'S ALL. HANNAH NEEDED HER HELP...
WELL... MAYBE HARBORING A BABY HAWK WASN'T THE BEST IDEA.
FAWN, I KNOW YOU. YOU'VE ALWAYS LET YOUR HEART GUIDE YOU, WHICH IS ADMIRABLE, BUT...
BUT I ALSO NEED TO LISTEN WITH MY HEAD.
NEXT TIME... I PROMISE I WILL.
OKAY, HANNAH-BANANA. NOW LET'S GIVE THAT WING A TRY!
SWOOSH

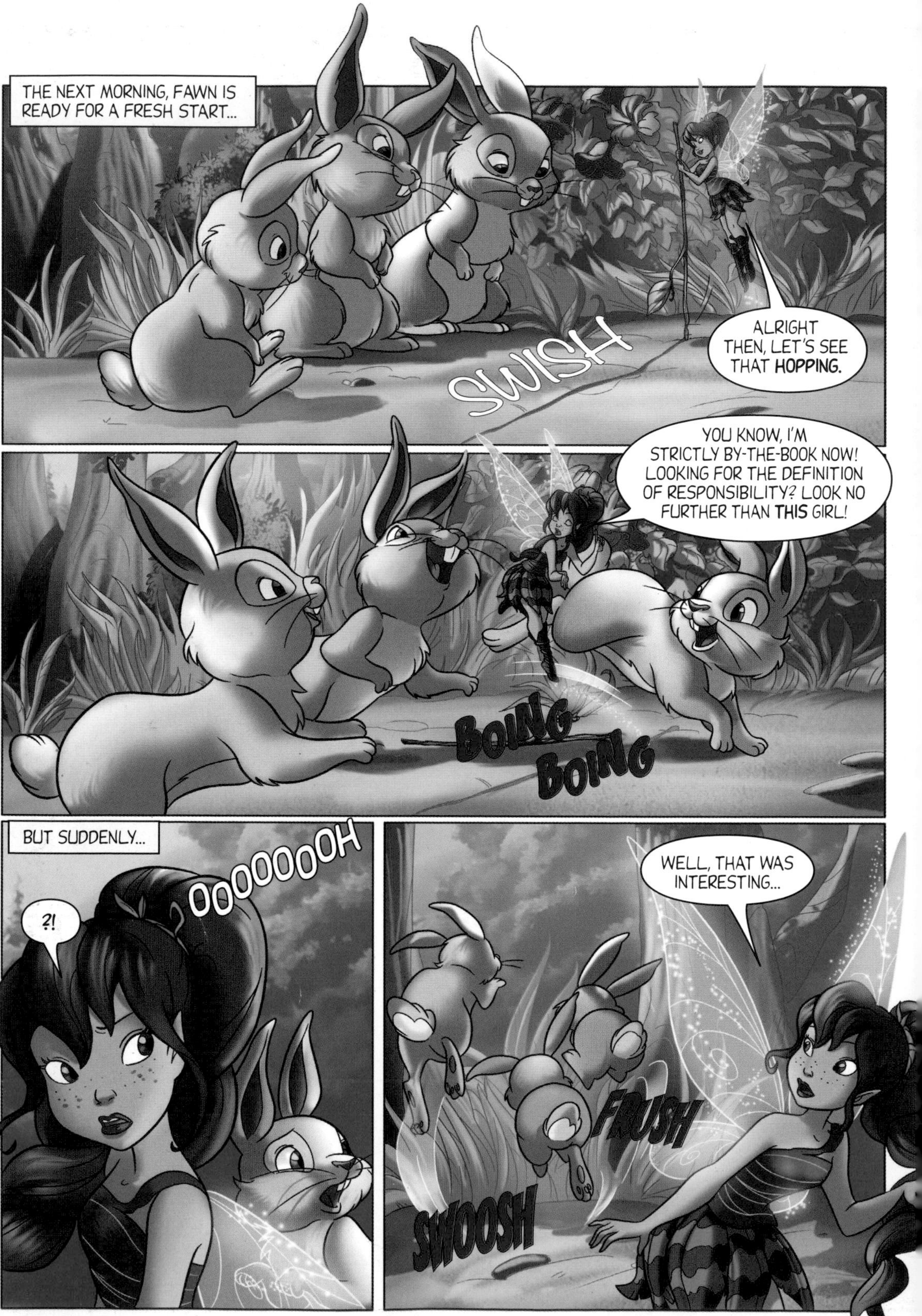

THE NEXT MORNING, FAWN IS READY FOR A FRESH START...
SWISH
ALRIGHT THEN, LET'S SEE THAT **HOPPING.**
YOU KNOW, I'M STRICTLY BY-THE-BOOK NOW! LOOKING FOR THE DEFINITION OF RESPONSIBILITY? LOOK NO FURTHER THAN **THIS** GIRL!
BOING
BOING
BUT SUDDENLY...
OOOOOOOOH
?!
WELL, THAT WAS INTERESTING...
FRUSH
SWOOSH

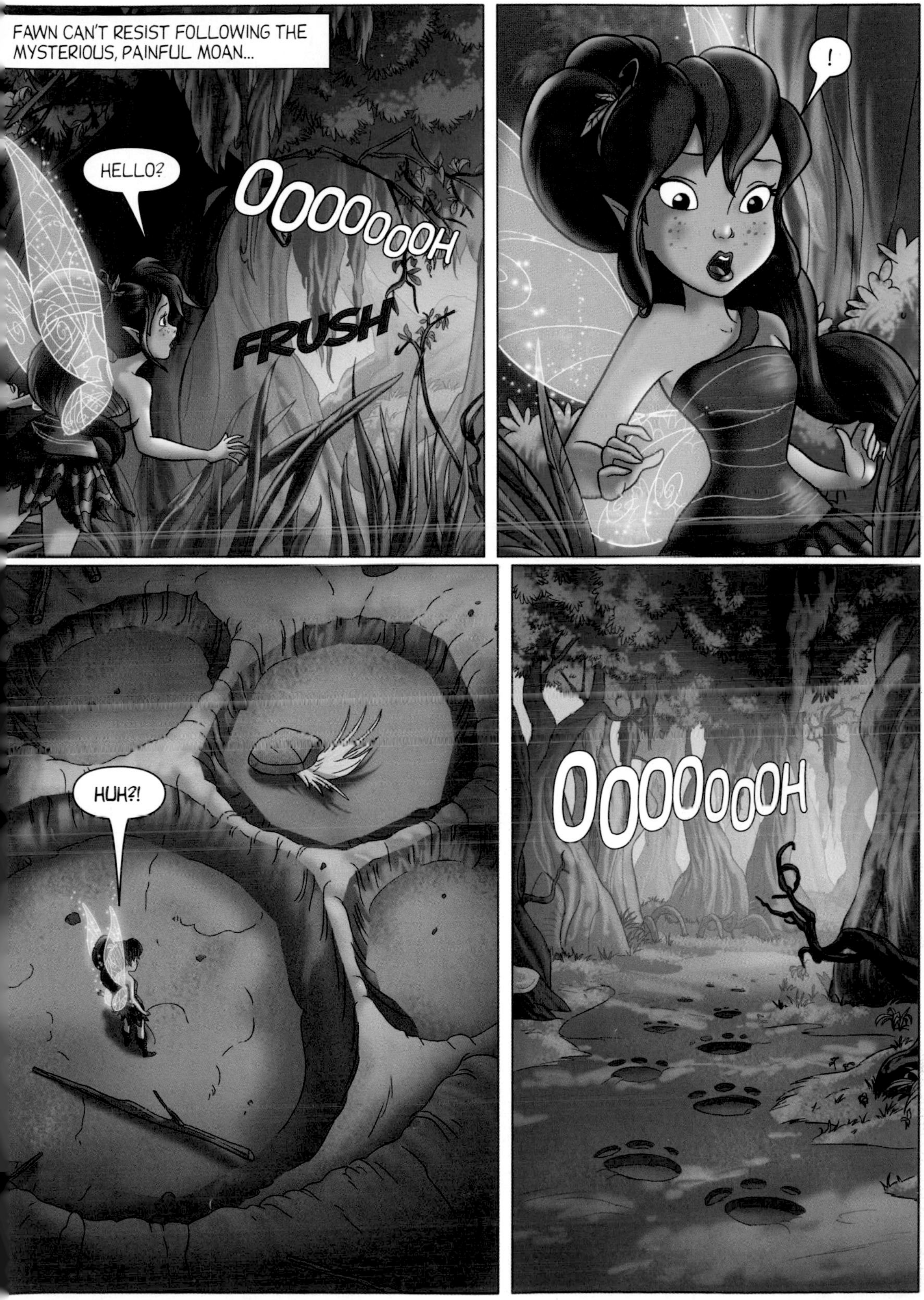

FAWN CAN'T RESIST FOLLOWING THE MYSTERIOUS, PAINFUL MOAN...
HELLO?
OOOOOOOOH
FRUSH
!
HUH?!
OOOOOOOOH

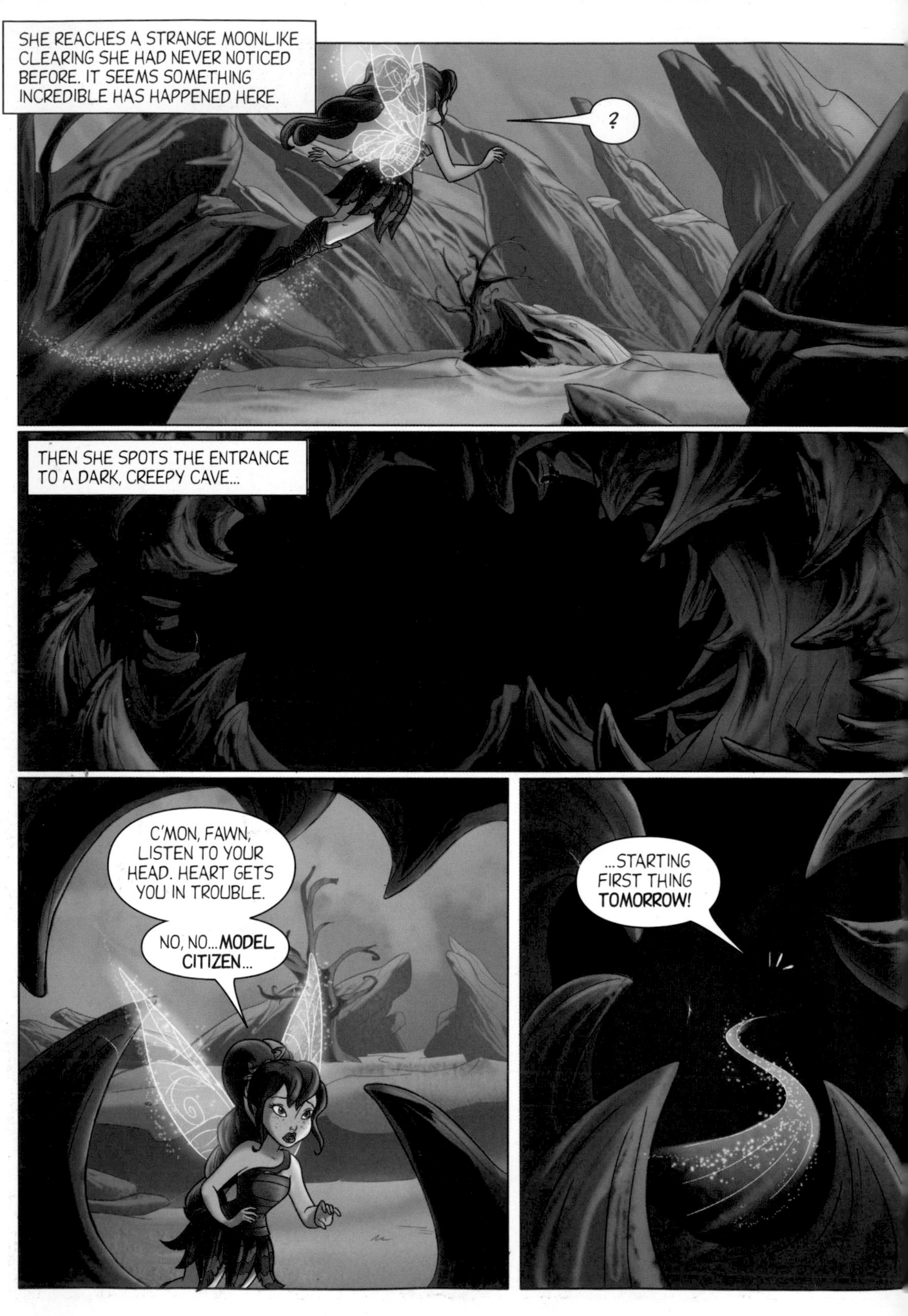
SHE REACHES A STRANGE MOONLIKE CLEARING SHE HAD NEVER NOTICED BEFORE. IT SEEMS SOMETHING INCREDIBLE HAS HAPPENED HERE.
?
THEN SHE SPOTS THE ENTRANCE TO A DARK, CREEPY CAVE...
C'MON, FAWN, LISTEN TO YOUR HEAD. HEART GETS YOU IN TROUBLE.
NO, NO... **MODEL CITIZEN**...
...STARTING FIRST THING **TOMORROW!**

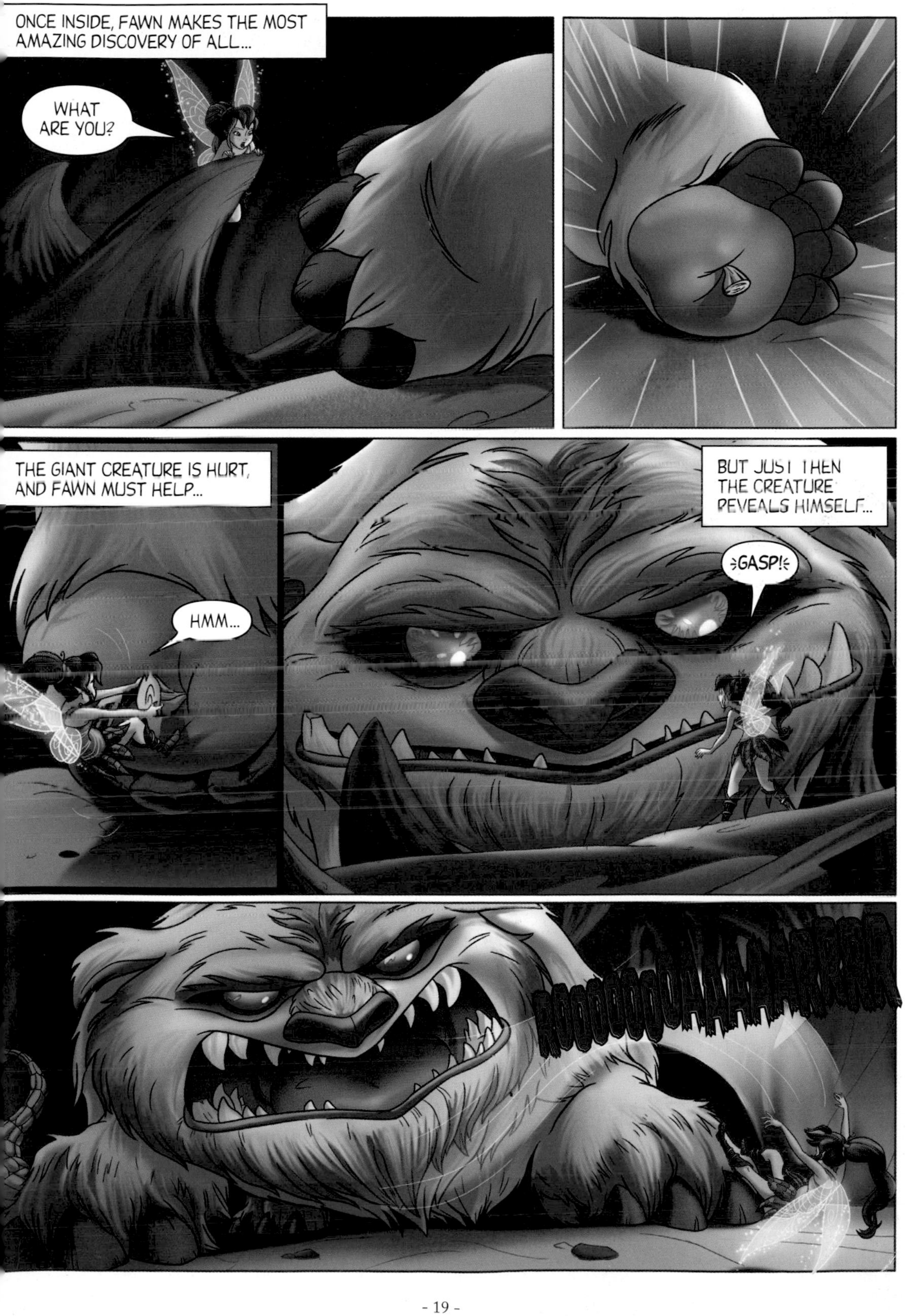
ONCE INSIDE, FAWN MAKES THE MOST AMAZING DISCOVERY OF ALL...
WHAT ARE YOU?
THE GIANT CREATURE IS HURT, AND FAWN MUST HELP...
HMM...
BUT JUST THEN THE CREATURE REVEALS HIMSELF...
GASP!
ROOOOOOOAAAAARRRR

PART TWO:

"Welcome, Gruff!"

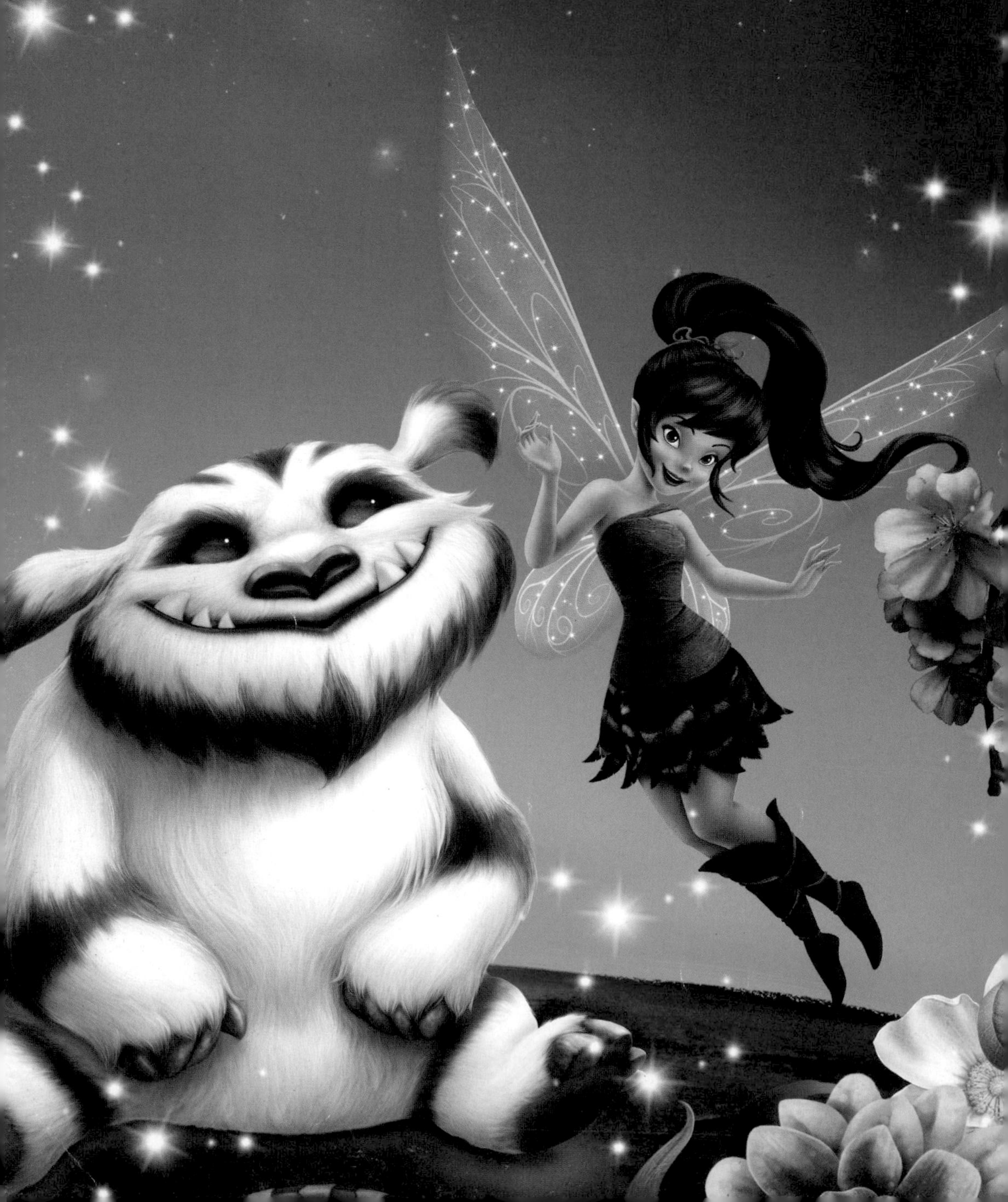

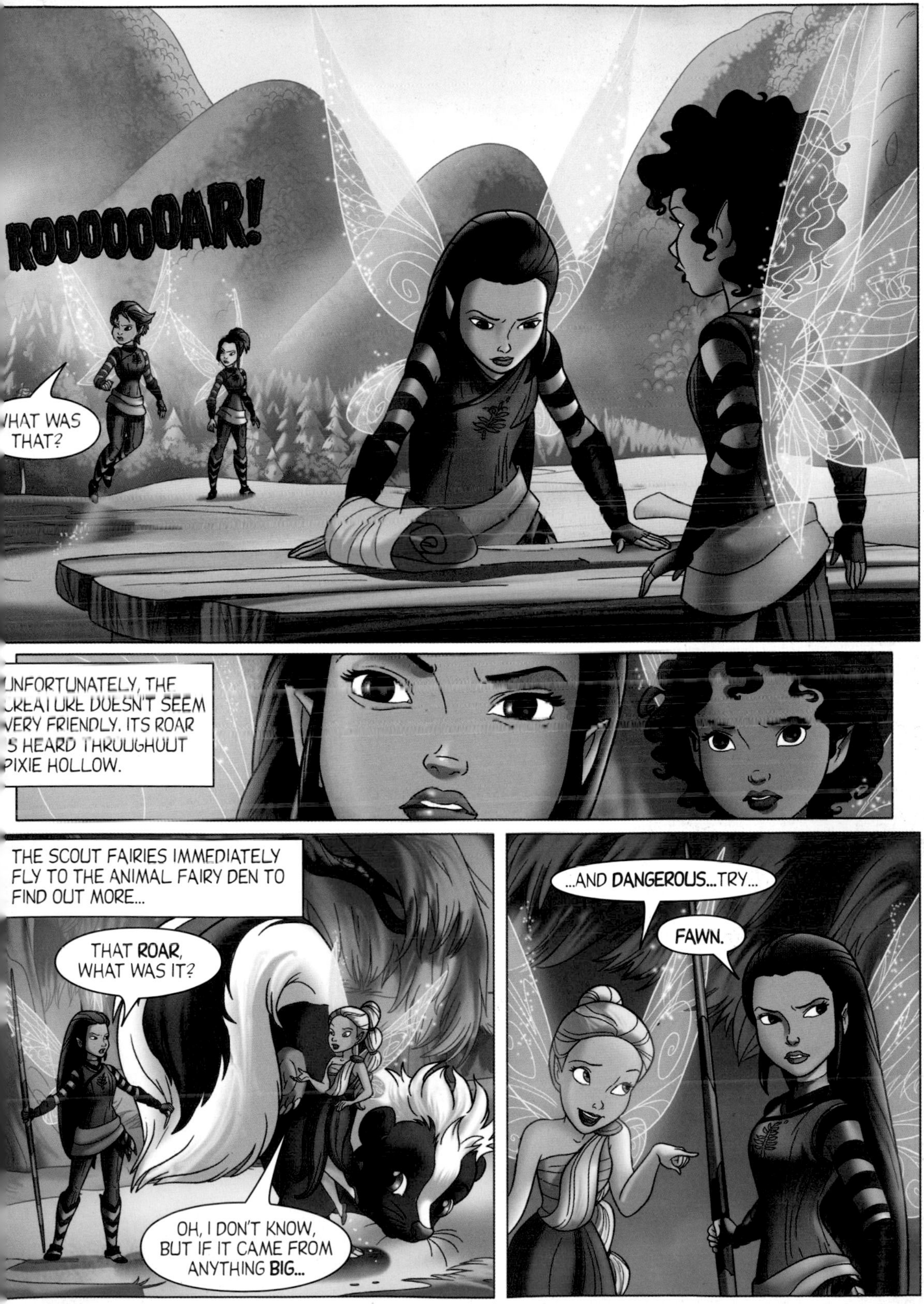
ROOOOOOOAR!
WHAT WAS THAT?
UNFORTUNATELY, THE CREATURE DOESN'T SEEM VERY FRIENDLY. ITS ROAR IS HEARD THROUGHOUT PIXIE HOLLOW.
THE SCOUT FAIRIES IMMEDIATELY FLY TO THE ANIMAL FAIRY DEN TO FIND OUT MORE...
THAT **ROAR**, WHAT WAS IT?
OH, I DON'T KNOW, BUT IF IT CAME FROM ANYTHING **BIG**...
...AND **DANGEROUS**...TRY...
FAWN.

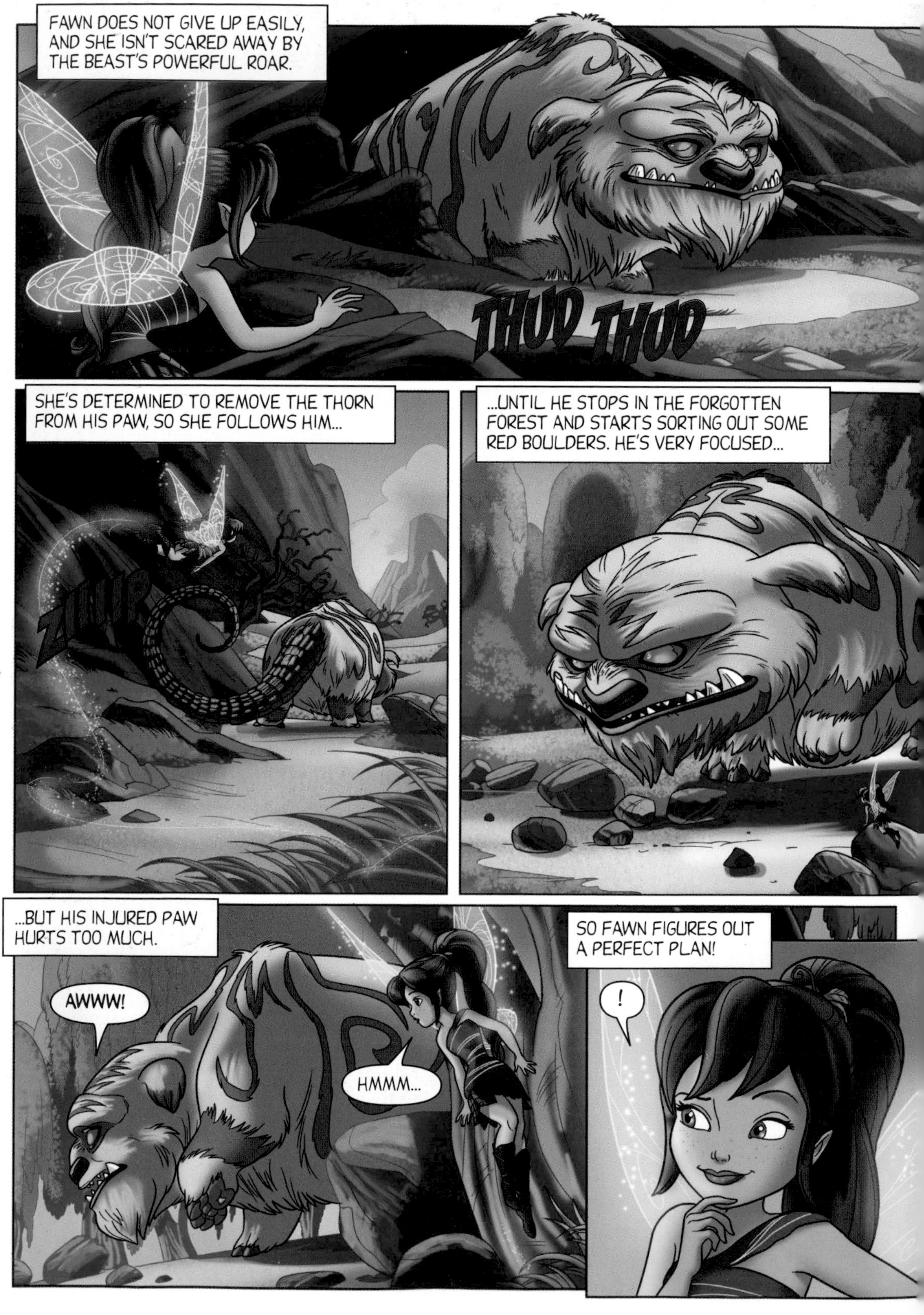
FAWN DOES NOT GIVE UP EASILY, AND SHE ISN'T SCARED AWAY BY THE BEAST'S POWERFUL ROAR.
THUD THUD
SHE'S DETERMINED TO REMOVE THE THORN FROM HIS PAW, SO SHE FOLLOWS HIM...
ZIIIIP
...UNTIL HE STOPS IN THE FORGOTTEN FOREST AND STARTS SORTING OUT SOME RED BOULDERS. HE'S VERY FOCUSED...
...BUT HIS INJURED PAW HURTS TOO MUCH.
AWWW!
HMMM...
SO FAWN FIGURES OUT A PERFECT PLAN!
!

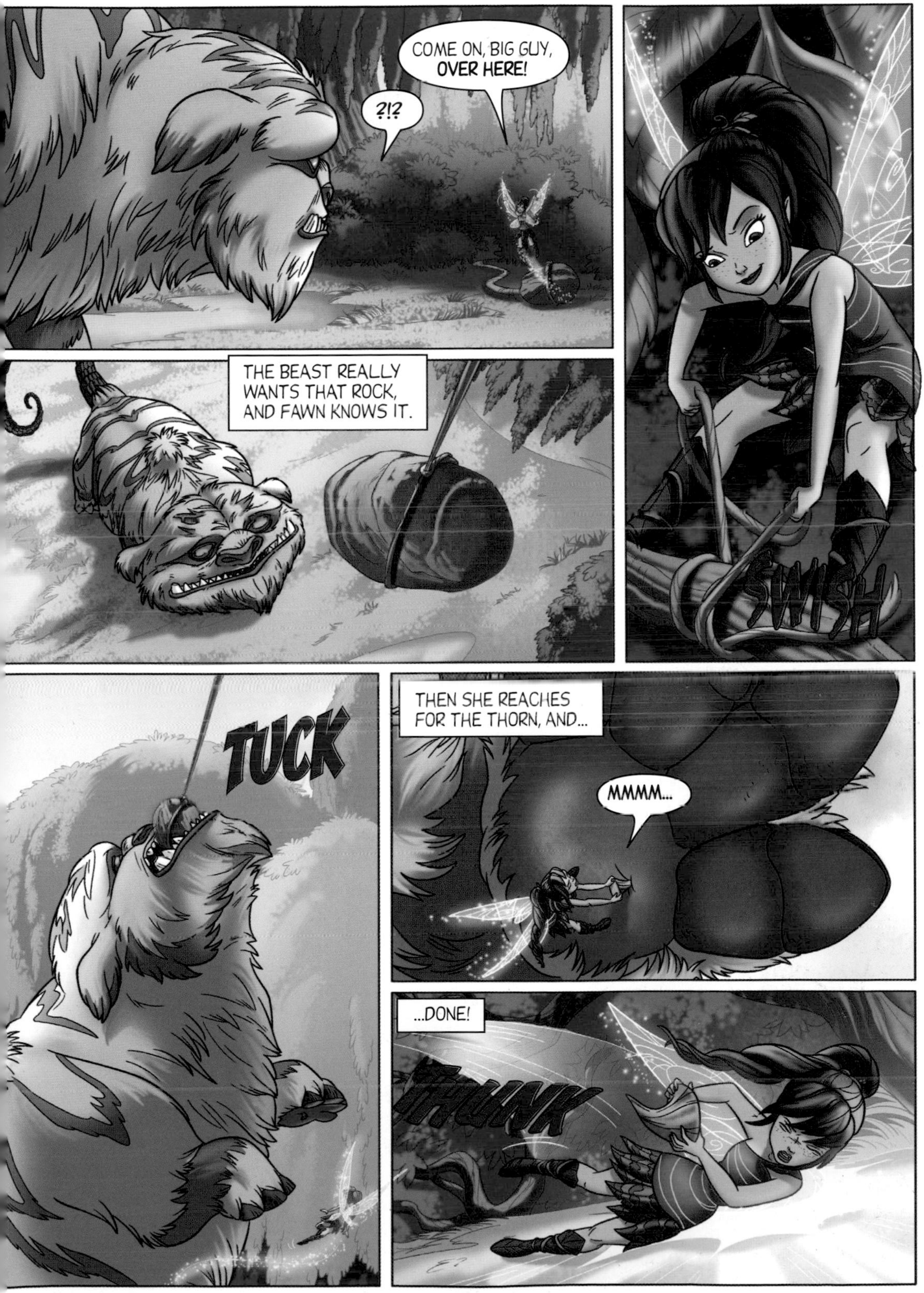

COME ON, BIG GUY, OVER HERE!
?!?
THE BEAST REALLY WANTS THAT ROCK, AND FAWN KNOWS IT.
SWISH
TUCK
THEN SHE REACHES FOR THE THORN, AND...
MMMM...
...DONE!
THUNK

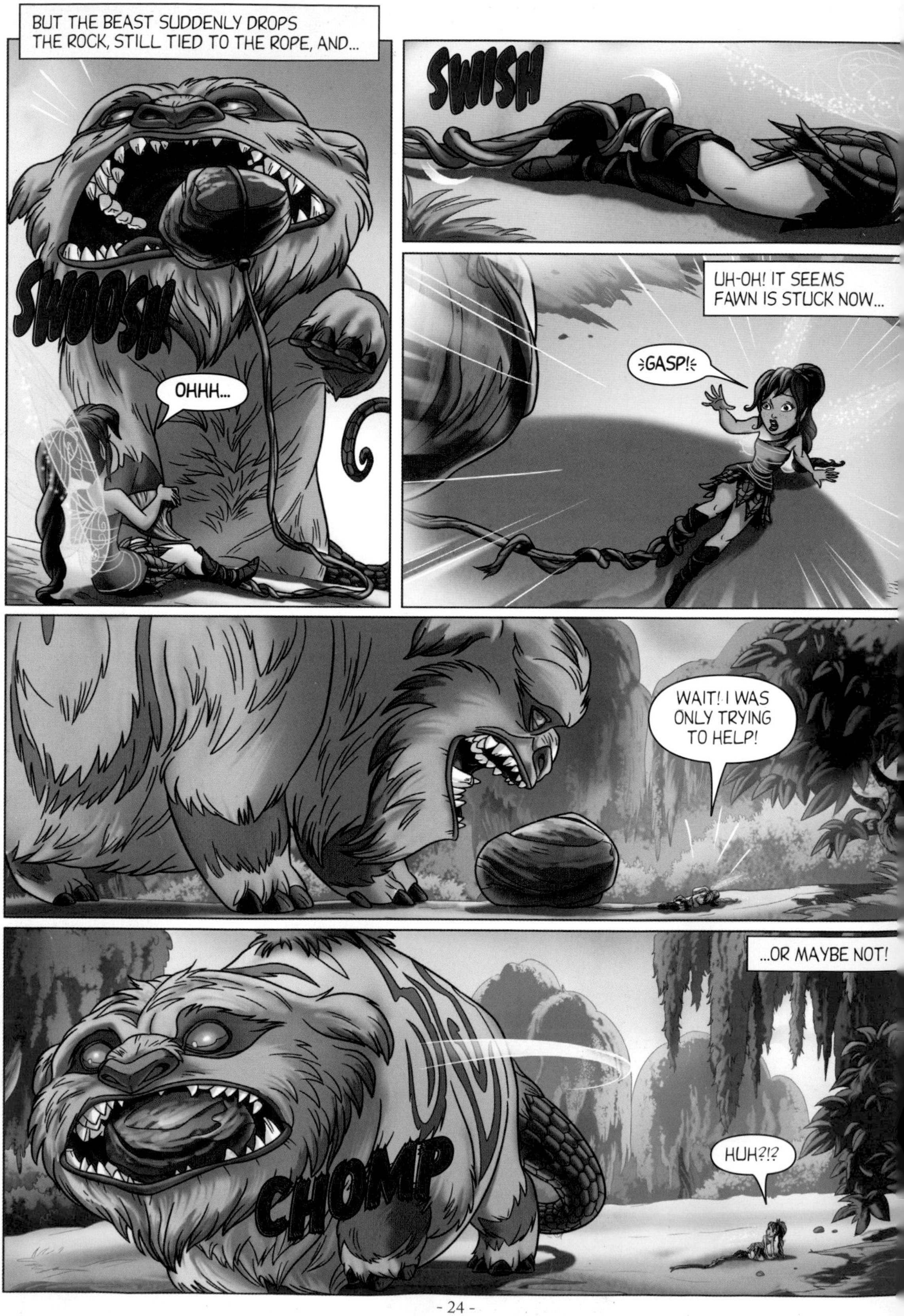

BUT THE BEAST SUDDENLY DROPS THE ROCK, STILL TIED TO THE ROPE, AND...
SWOOSH
OHHH...
SWISH
UH-OH! IT SEEMS FAWN IS STUCK NOW...
GASP!
WAIT! I WAS ONLY TRYING TO HELP!
...OR MAYBE NOT!
CHOMP
HUH?!?

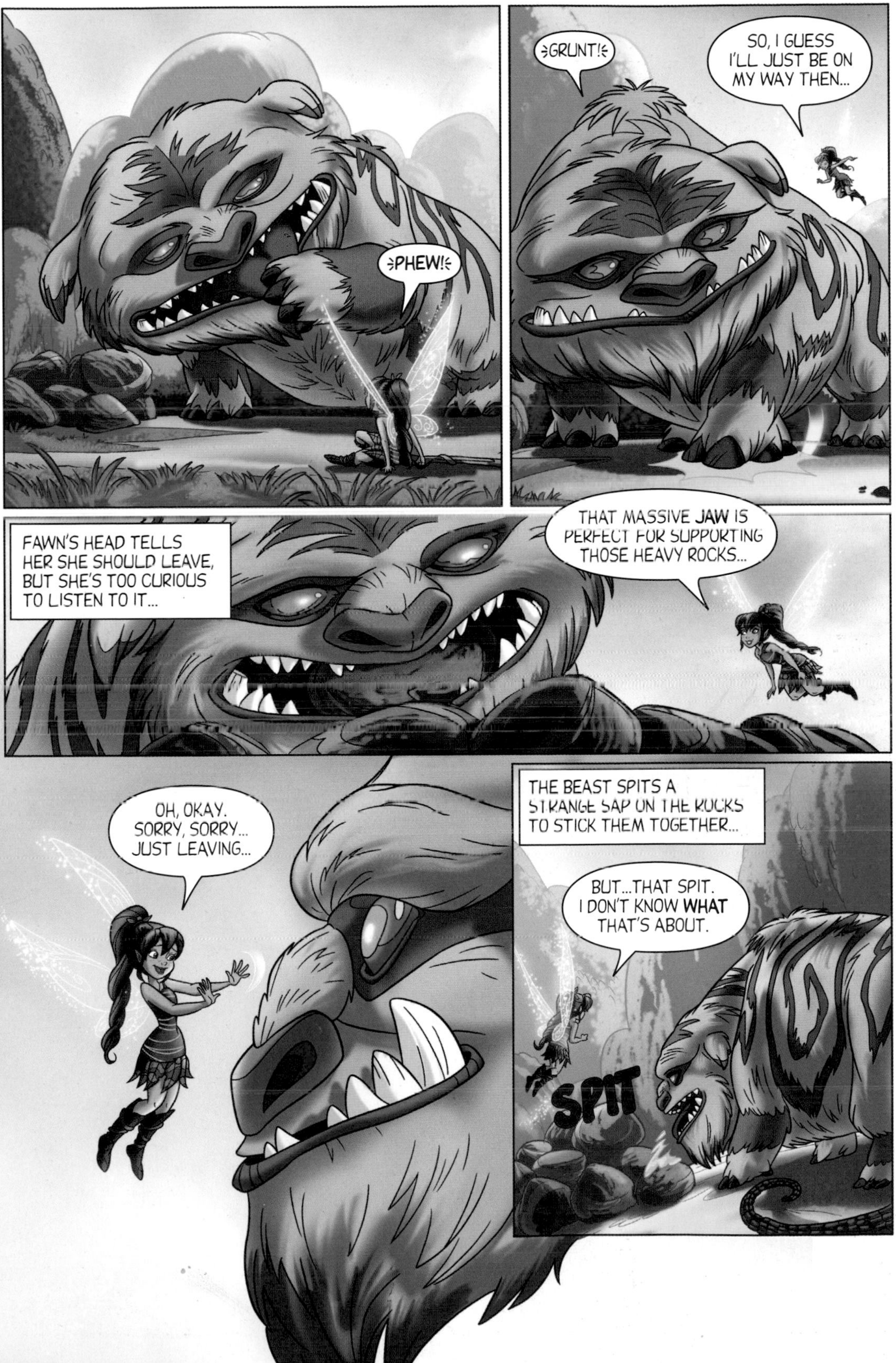
PHEW!
GRUNT!
SO, I GUESS I'LL JUST BE ON MY WAY THEN...
FAWN'S HEAD TELLS HER SHE SHOULD LEAVE, BUT SHE'S TOO CURIOUS TO LISTEN TO IT...
THAT MASSIVE **JAW** IS PERFECT FOR SUPPORTING THOSE HEAVY ROCKS...
OH, OKAY. SORRY, SORRY... JUST LEAVING...
THE BEAST SPITS A STRANGE SAP ON THE ROCKS TO STICK THEM TOGETHER...
BUT...THAT SPIT. I DON'T KNOW **WHAT** THAT'S ABOUT.
SPIT

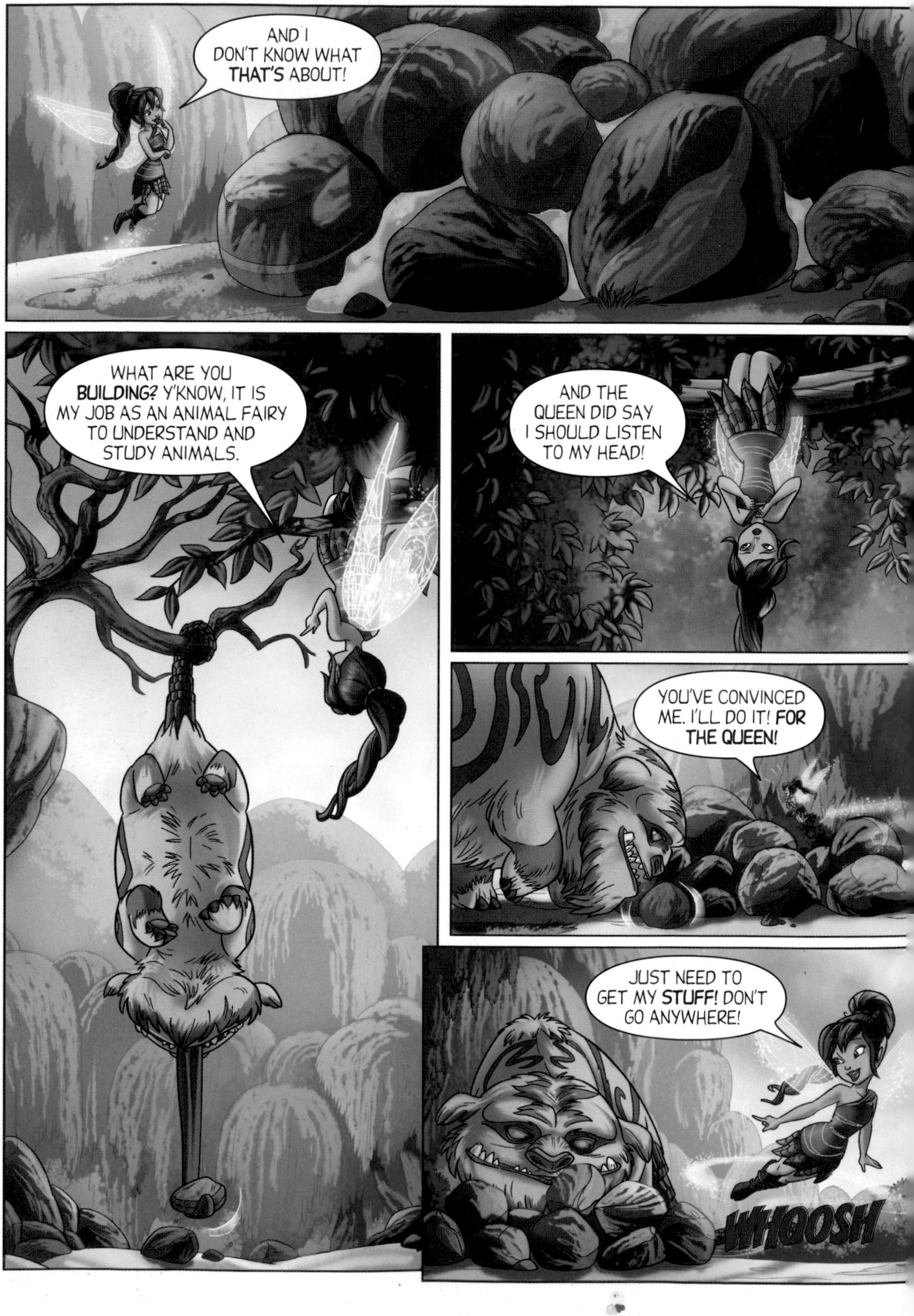
AND I DON'T KNOW WHAT **THAT'S** ABOUT!
WHAT ARE YOU **BUILDING?** Y'KNOW, IT IS MY JOB AS AN ANIMAL FAIRY TO UNDERSTAND AND STUDY ANIMALS.
AND THE QUEEN DID SAY I SHOULD LISTEN TO MY HEAD!
YOU'VE CONVINCED ME. I'LL DO IT! **FOR THE QUEEN!**
JUST NEED TO GET MY **STUFF!** DON'T GO ANYWHERE!
WHOOSH

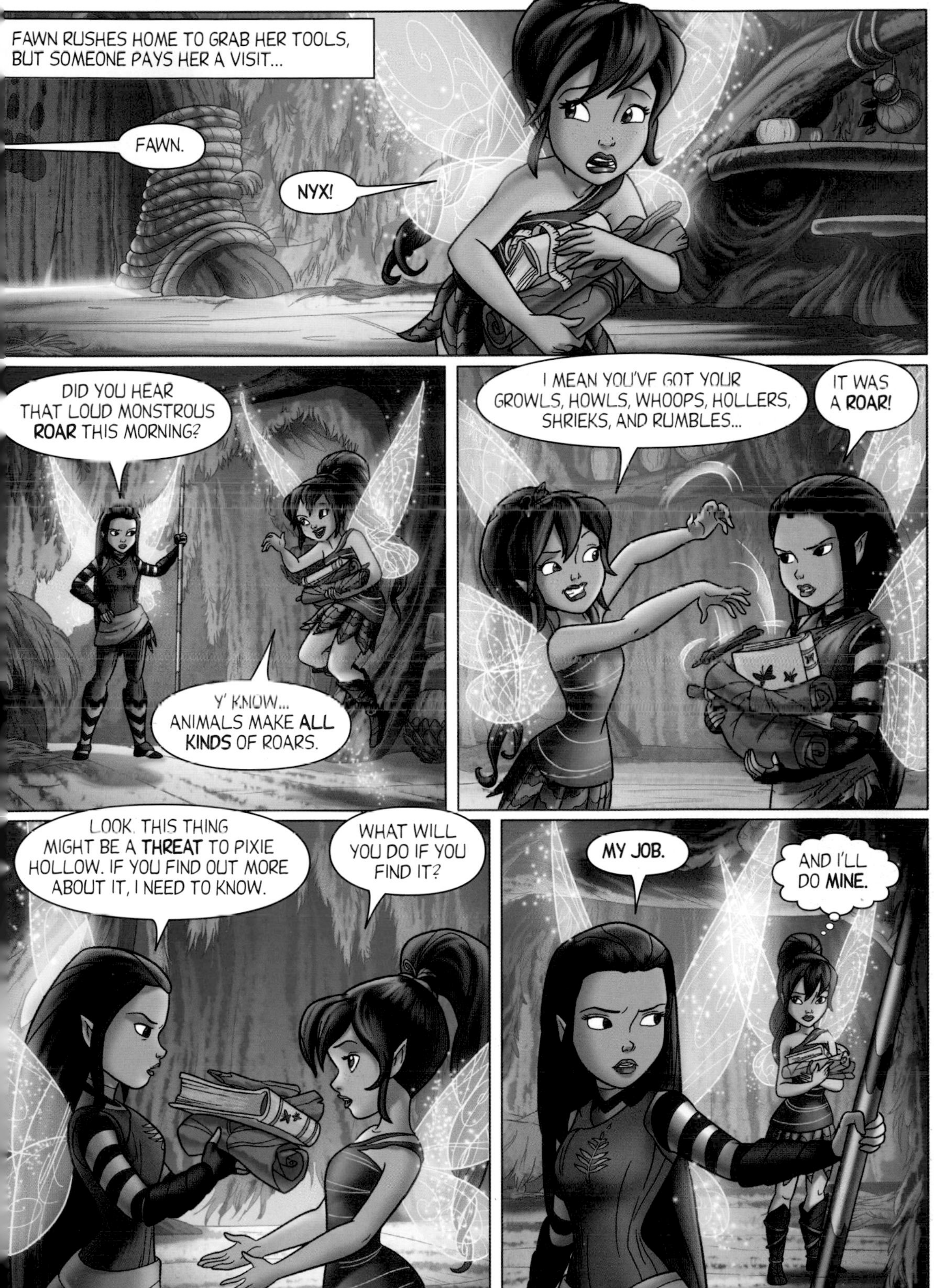

FAWN RUSHES HOME TO GRAB HER TOOLS, BUT SOMEONE PAYS HER A VISIT...
FAWN.
NYX!
DID YOU HEAR THAT LOUD MONSTROUS **ROAR** THIS MORNING?
Y' KNOW... ANIMALS MAKE **ALL KINDS** OF ROARS.
I MEAN YOU'VE GOT YOUR GROWLS, HOWLS, WHOOPS, HOLLERS, SHRIEKS, AND RUMBLES...
IT WAS A **ROAR!**
LOOK. THIS THING MIGHT BE A **THREAT** TO PIXIE HOLLOW. IF YOU FIND OUT MORE ABOUT IT, I NEED TO KNOW.
WHAT WILL YOU DO IF YOU FIND IT?
MY JOB.
AND I'LL DO **MINE.**

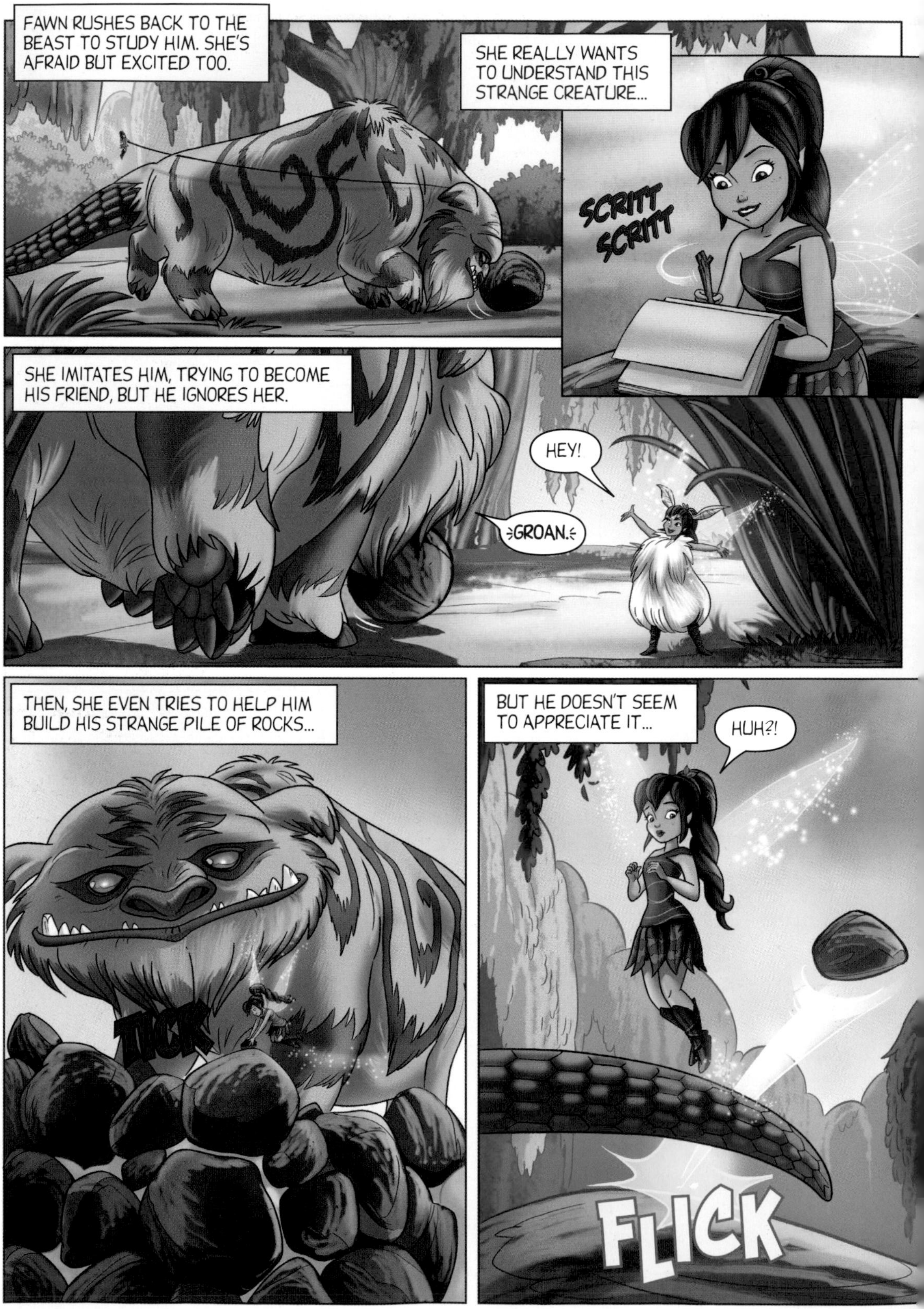
FAWN RUSHES BACK TO THE BEAST TO STUDY HIM. SHE'S AFRAID BUT EXCITED TOO.
SHE REALLY WANTS TO UNDERSTAND THIS STRANGE CREATURE...
SCRITT SCRITT
SHE IMITATES HIM, TRYING TO BECOME HIS FRIEND, BUT HE IGNORES HER.
HEY!
GROAN.
THEN, SHE EVEN TRIES TO HELP HIM BUILD HIS STRANGE PILE OF ROCKS...
TICK
BUT HE DOESN'T SEEM TO APPRECIATE IT...
HUH?!
FLICK

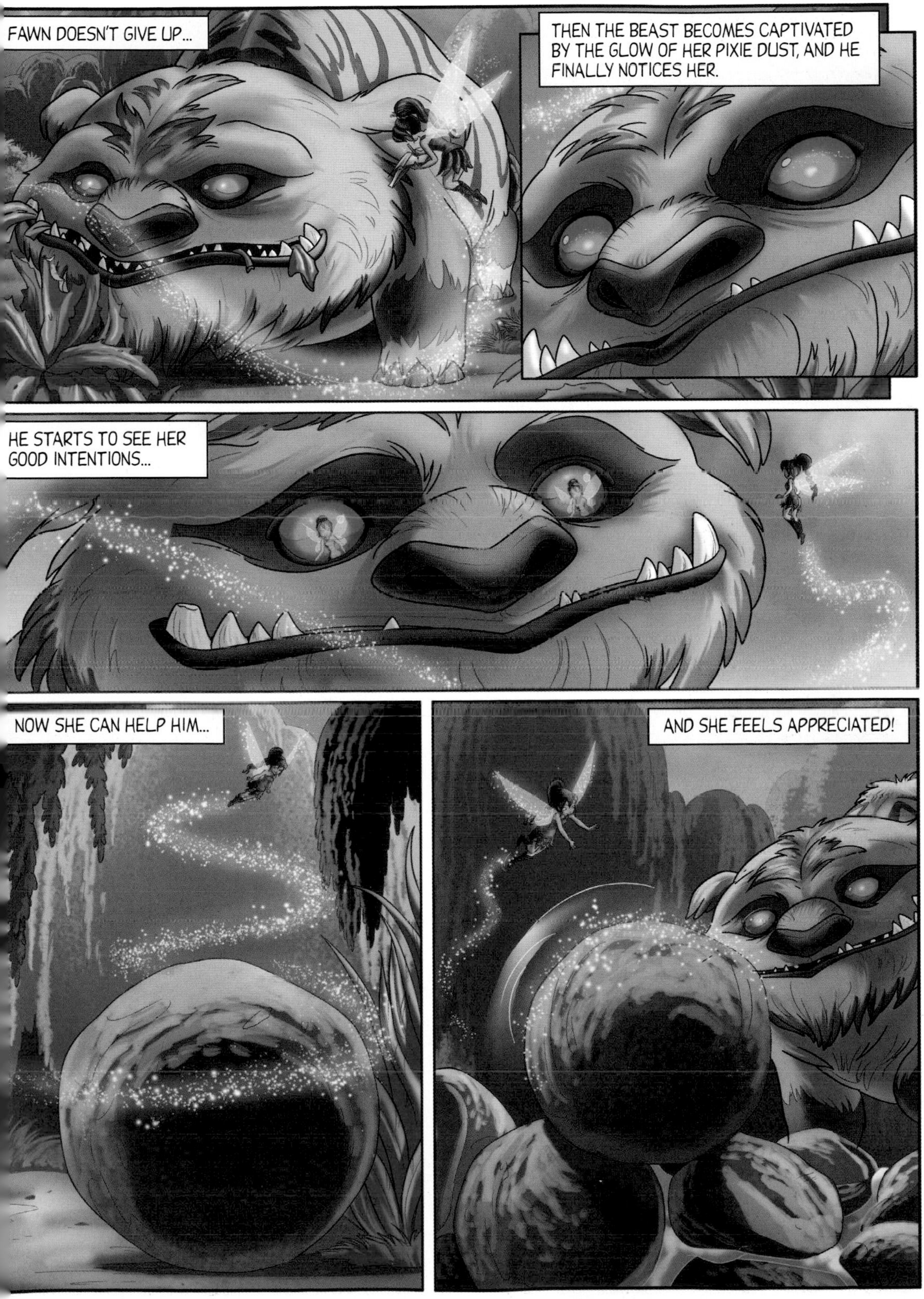
FAWN DOESN'T GIVE UP...
THEN THE BEAST BECOMES CAPTIVATED BY THE GLOW OF HER PIXIE DUST, AND HE FINALLY NOTICES HER.
HE STARTS TO SEE HER GOOD INTENTIONS...
NOW SHE CAN HELP HIM...
AND SHE FEELS APPRECIATED!

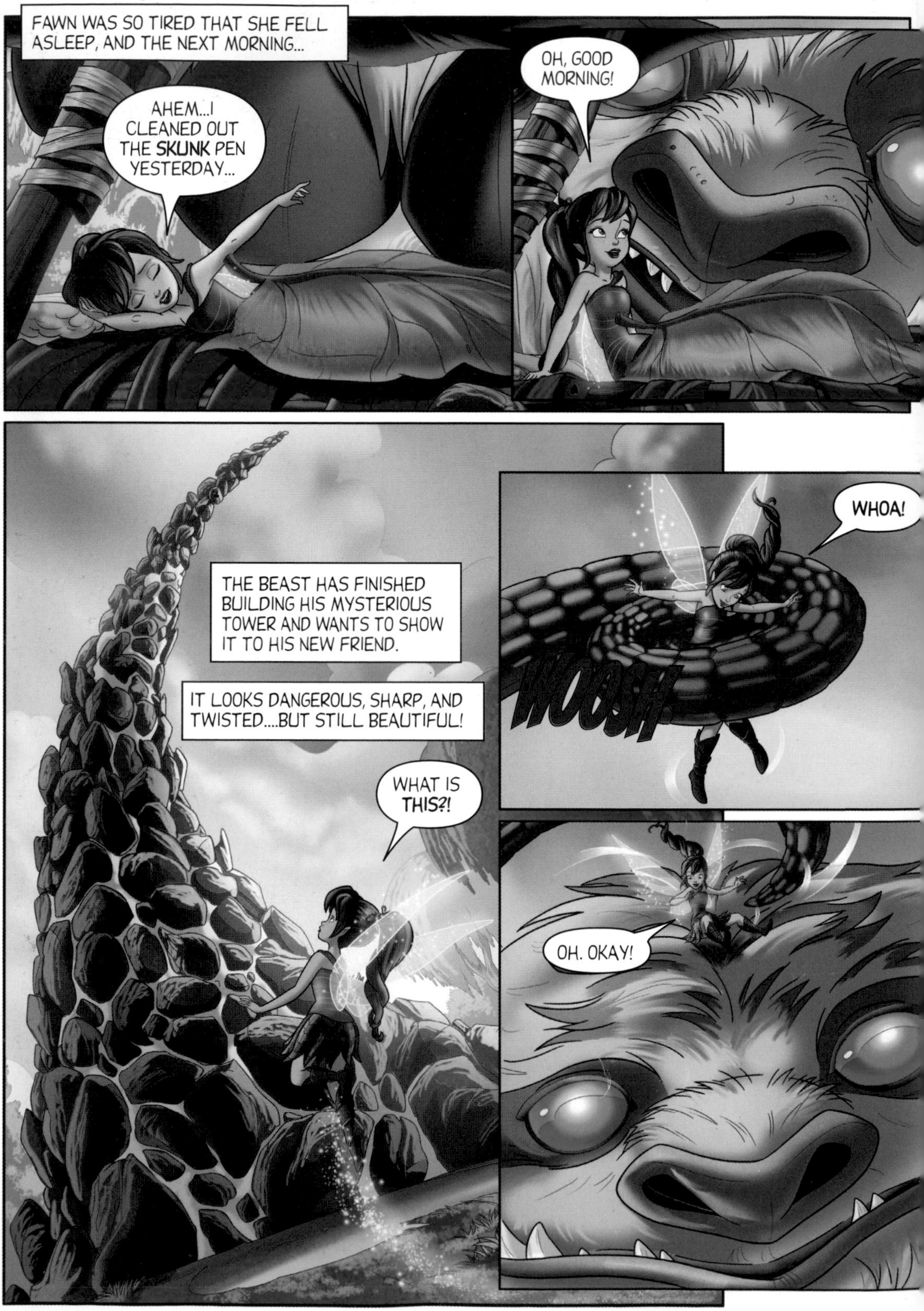
FAWN WAS SO TIRED THAT SHE FELL ASLEEP, AND THE NEXT MORNING...
AHEM...I CLEANED OUT THE SKUNK PEN YESTERDAY...
OH, GOOD MORNING!
THE BEAST HAS FINISHED BUILDING HIS MYSTERIOUS TOWER AND WANTS TO SHOW IT TO HIS NEW FRIEND.
IT LOOKS DANGEROUS, SHARP, AND TWISTED....BUT STILL BEAUTIFUL!
WHAT IS THIS?!
WHOA!
WOOSH
OH. OKAY!

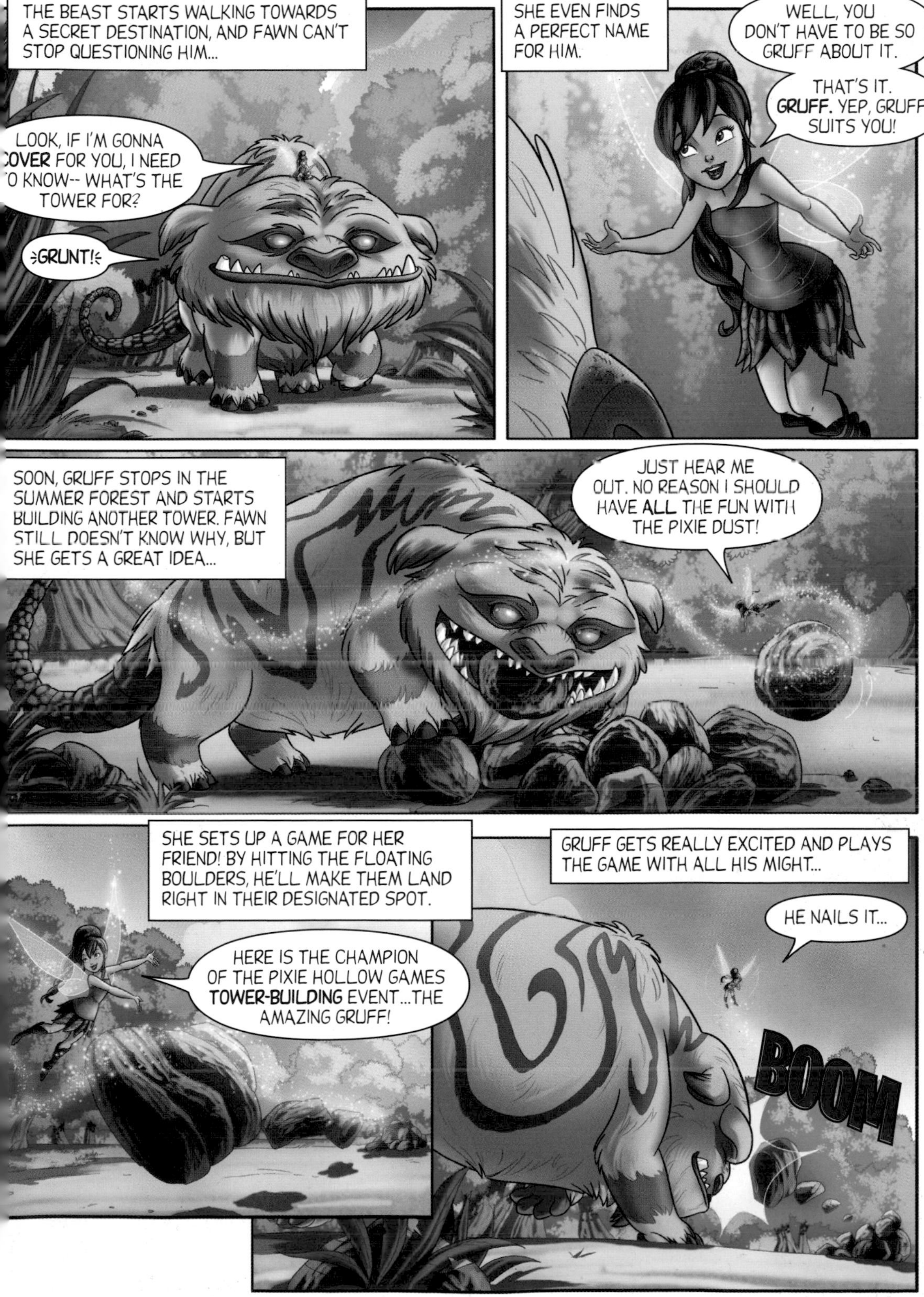
THE BEAST STARTS WALKING TOWARDS A SECRET DESTINATION, AND FAWN CAN'T STOP QUESTIONING HIM...
LOOK, IF I'M GONNA COVER FOR YOU, I NEED O KNOW-- WHAT'S THE TOWER FOR?
GRUNT!
SHE EVEN FINDS A PERFECT NAME FOR HIM.
WELL, YOU DON'T HAVE TO BE SO GRUFF ABOUT IT.
THAT'S IT. GRUFF. YEP, GRUFF SUITS YOU!
SOON, GRUFF STOPS IN THE SUMMER FOREST AND STARTS BUILDING ANOTHER TOWER. FAWN STILL DOESN'T KNOW WHY, BUT SHE GETS A GREAT IDEA...
JUST HEAR ME OUT. NO REASON I SHOULD HAVE ALL THE FUN WITH THE PIXIE DUST!
SHE SETS UP A GAME FOR HER FRIEND! BY HITTING THE FLOATING BOULDERS, HE'LL MAKE THEM LAND RIGHT IN THEIR DESIGNATED SPOT.
HERE IS THE CHAMPION OF THE PIXIE HOLLOW GAMES TOWER-BUILDING EVENT...THE AMAZING GRUFF!
GRUFF GETS REALLY EXCITED AND PLAYS THE GAME WITH ALL HIS MIGHT...
HE NAILS IT...
BOOM

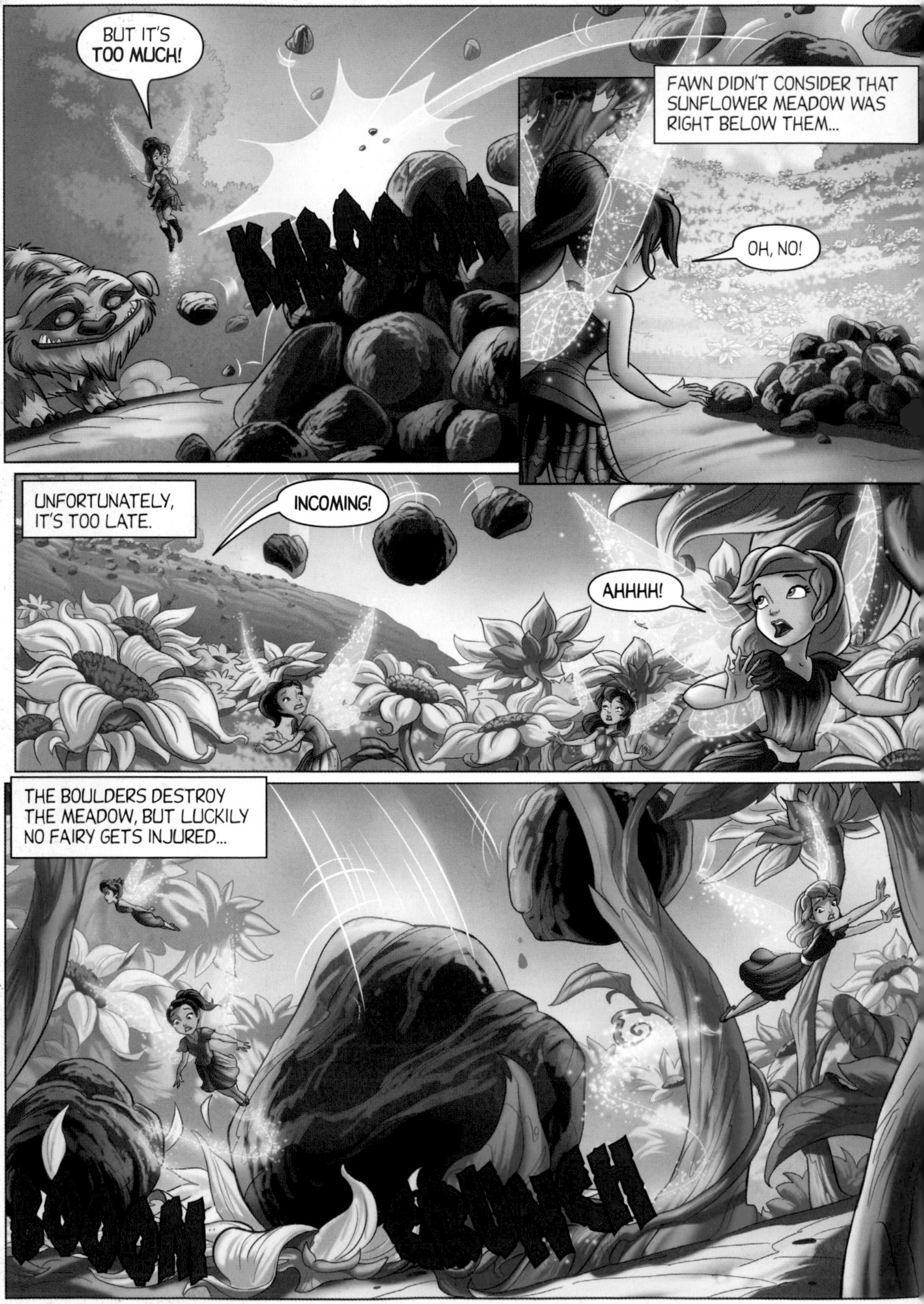
BUT IT'S TOO MUCH!
FAWN DIDN'T CONSIDER THAT SUNFLOWER MEADOW WAS RIGHT BELOW THEM...
OH, NO!
UNFORTUNATELY, IT'S TOO LATE.
INCOMING!
AHHHH!
THE BOULDERS DESTROY THE MEADOW, BUT LUCKILY NO FAIRY GETS INJURED...

PART THREE: "All Together Now"

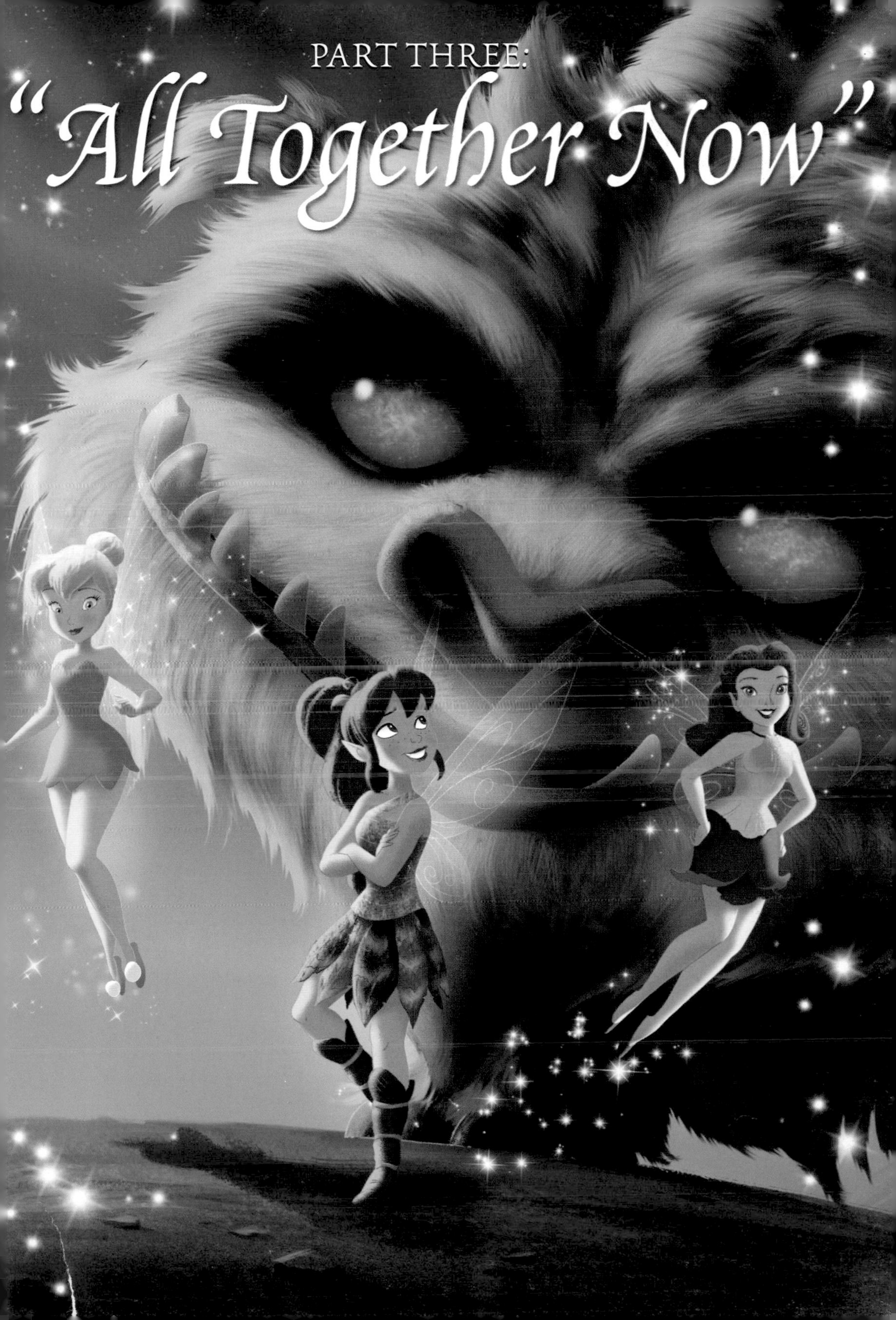

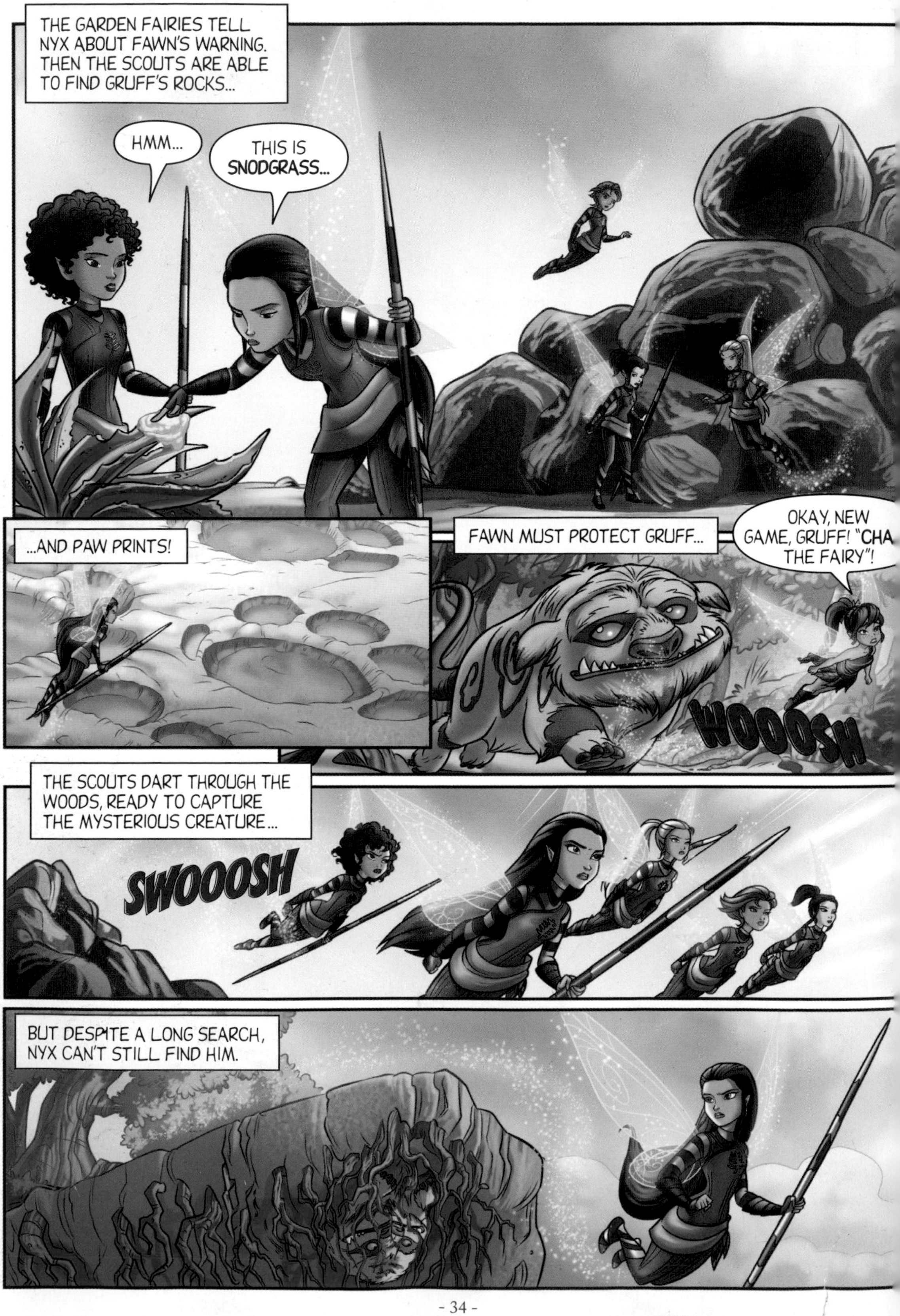
THE GARDEN FAIRIES TELL NYX ABOUT FAWN'S WARNING. THEN THE SCOUTS ARE ABLE TO FIND GRUFF'S ROCKS...
HMM...
THIS IS SNODGRASS...
...AND PAW PRINTS!
FAWN MUST PROTECT GRUFF...
OKAY, NEW GAME, GRUFF! "CHA THE FAIRY"!
WOOOSH
THE SCOUTS DART THROUGH THE WOODS, READY TO CAPTURE THE MYSTERIOUS CREATURE...
SWOOOSH
BUT DESPITE A LONG SEARCH, NYX CAN'T STILL FIND HIM.

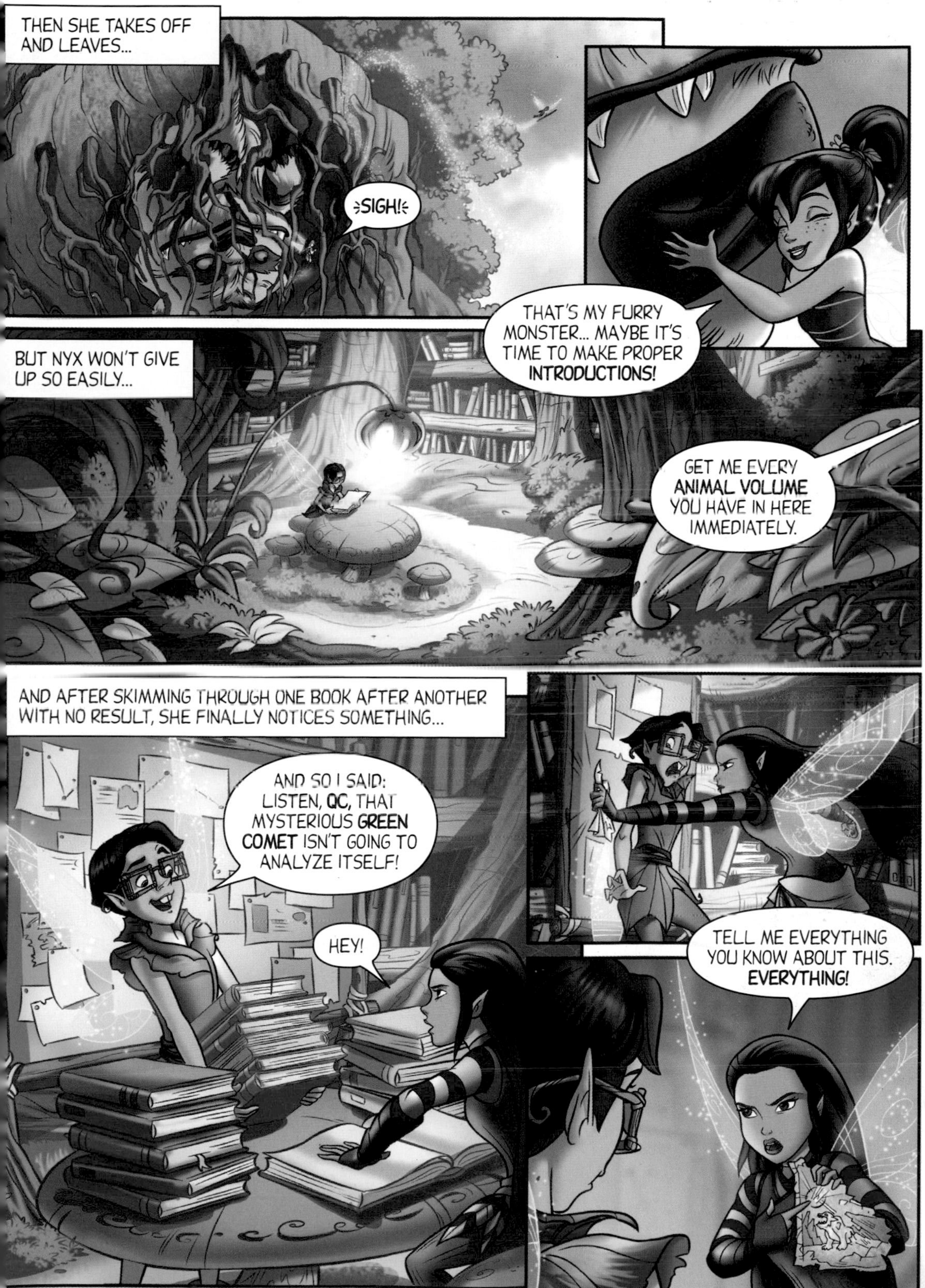
THEN SHE TAKES OFF AND LEAVES...
SIGH!
THAT'S MY FURRY MONSTER... MAYBE IT'S TIME TO MAKE PROPER INTRODUCTIONS!
BUT NYX WON'T GIVE UP SO EASILY...
GET ME EVERY ANIMAL VOLUME YOU HAVE IN HERE IMMEDIATELY.
AND AFTER SKIMMING THROUGH ONE BOOK AFTER ANOTHER WITH NO RESULT, SHE FINALLY NOTICES SOMETHING...
AND SO I SAID: LISTEN, QC, THAT MYSTERIOUS GREEN COMET ISN'T GOING TO ANALYZE ITSELF!
HEY!
TELL ME EVERYTHING YOU KNOW ABOUT THIS. EVERYTHING!

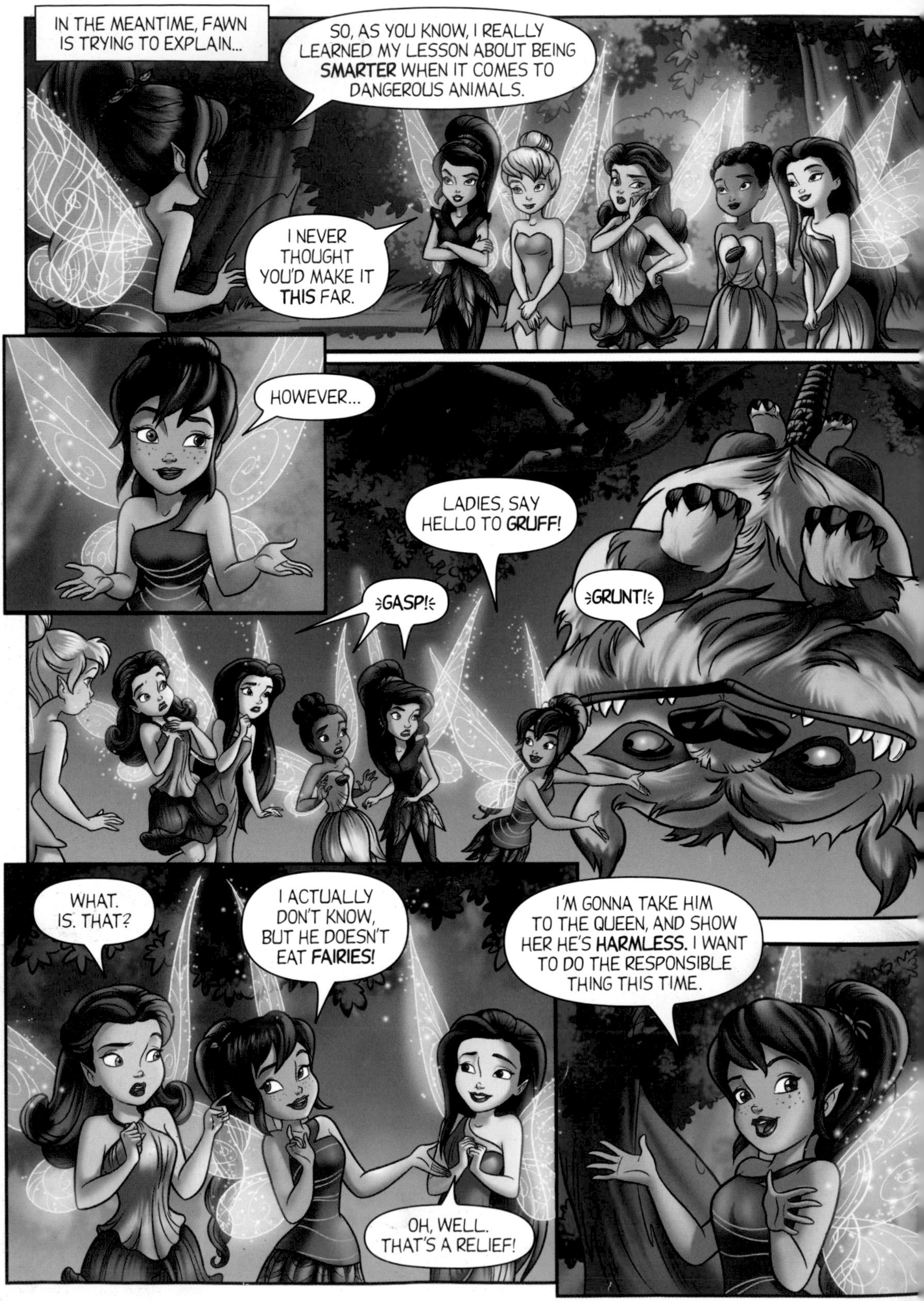

IN THE MEANTIME, FAWN IS TRYING TO EXPLAIN...
SO, AS YOU KNOW, I REALLY LEARNED MY LESSON ABOUT BEING SMARTER WHEN IT COMES TO DANGEROUS ANIMALS.
I NEVER THOUGHT YOU'D MAKE IT THIS FAR.
HOWEVER...
LADIES, SAY HELLO TO GRUFF!
GASP!
GRUNT!
WHAT. IS. THAT?
I ACTUALLY DON'T KNOW, BUT HE DOESN'T EAT FAIRIES!
OH, WELL. THAT'S A RELIEF!
I'M GONNA TAKE HIM TO THE QUEEN, AND SHOW HER HE'S HARMLESS. I WANT TO DO THE RESPONSIBLE THING THIS TIME.

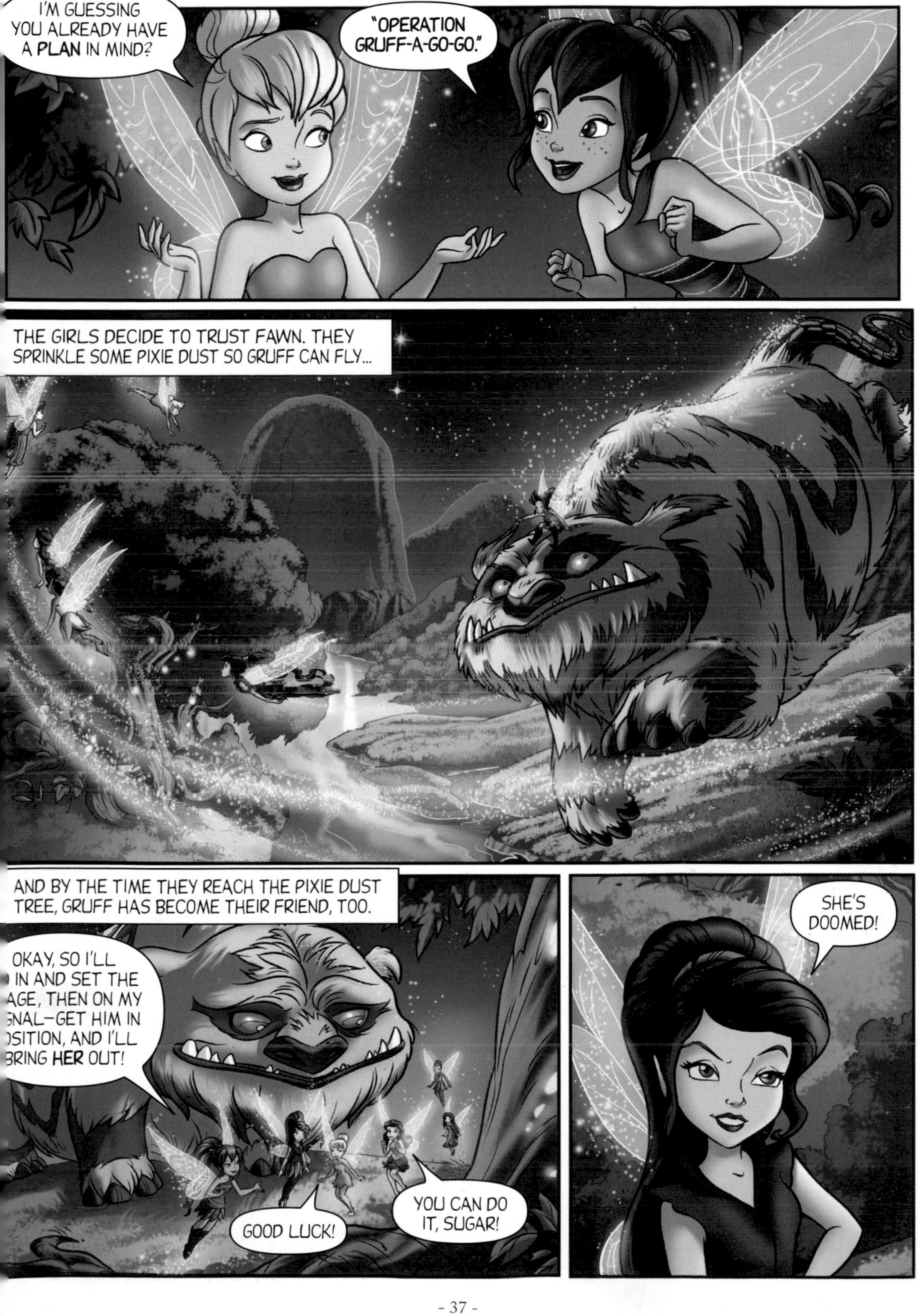
I'M GUESSING YOU ALREADY HAVE A **PLAN** IN MIND?
"OPERATION GRUFF-A-GO-GO."
THE GIRLS DECIDE TO TRUST FAWN. THEY SPRINKLE SOME PIXIE DUST SO GRUFF CAN FLY...
AND BY THE TIME THEY REACH THE PIXIE DUST TREE, GRUFF HAS BECOME THEIR FRIEND, TOO.
OKAY, SO I'LL IN AND SET THE AGE, THEN ON MY GNAL—GET HIM IN SITION, AND I'LL BRING **HER** OUT!
GOOD LUCK!
YOU CAN DO IT, SUGAR!
SHE'S DOOMED!

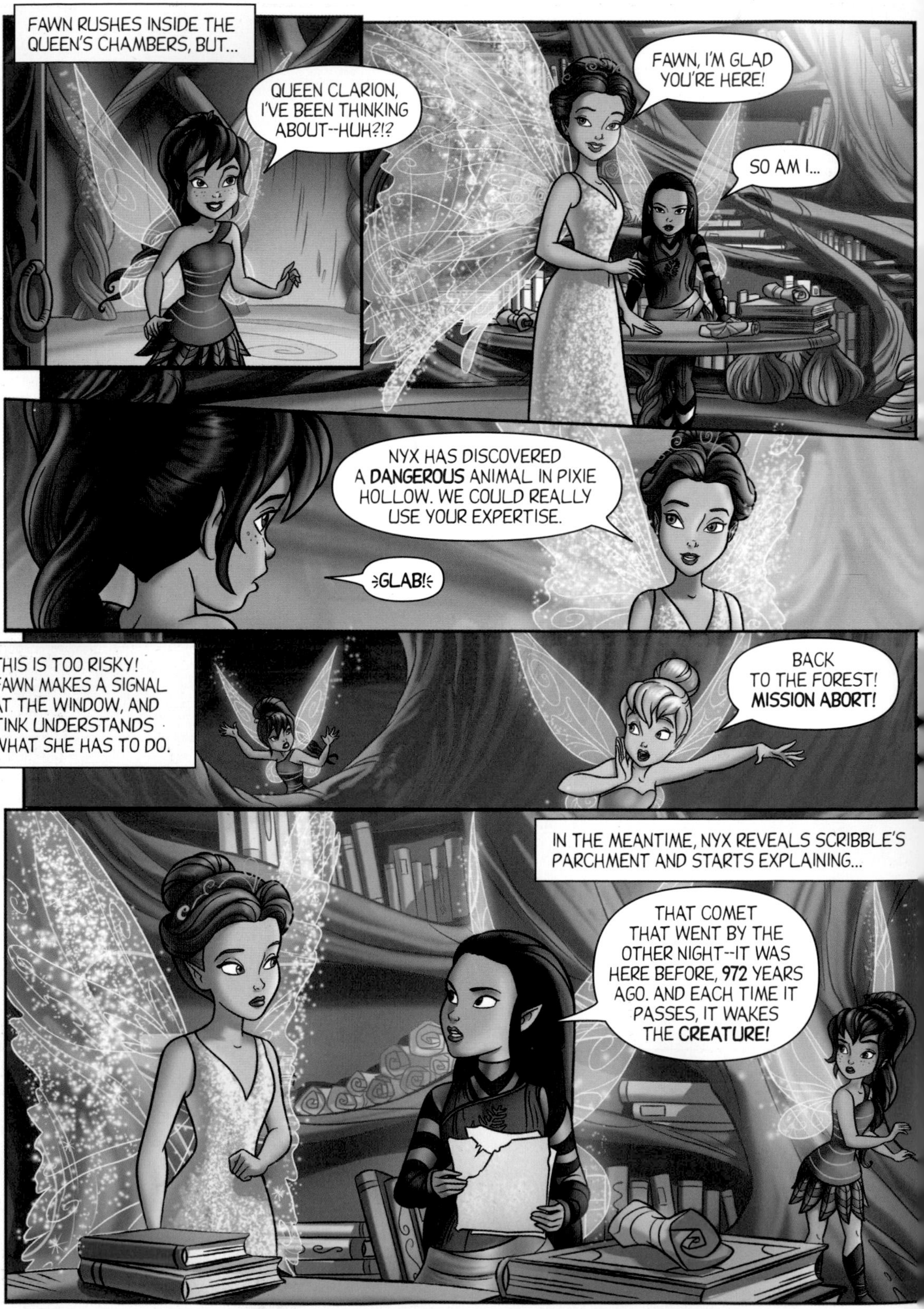
FAWN RUSHES INSIDE THE QUEEN'S CHAMBERS, BUT...
QUEEN CLARION, I'VE BEEN THINKING ABOUT--HUH?!?
FAWN, I'M GLAD YOU'RE HERE!
SO AM I...
NYX HAS DISCOVERED A DANGEROUS ANIMAL IN PIXIE HOLLOW. WE COULD REALLY USE YOUR EXPERTISE.
GLAB!
THIS IS TOO RISKY! FAWN MAKES A SIGNAL AT THE WINDOW, AND TINK UNDERSTANDS WHAT SHE HAS TO DO.
BACK TO THE FOREST! MISSION ABORT!
IN THE MEANTIME, NYX REVEALS SCRIBBLE'S PARCHMENT AND STARTS EXPLAINING...
THAT COMET THAT WENT BY THE OTHER NIGHT--IT WAS HERE BEFORE, 972 YEARS AGO. AND EACH TIME IT PASSES, IT WAKES THE CREATURE!

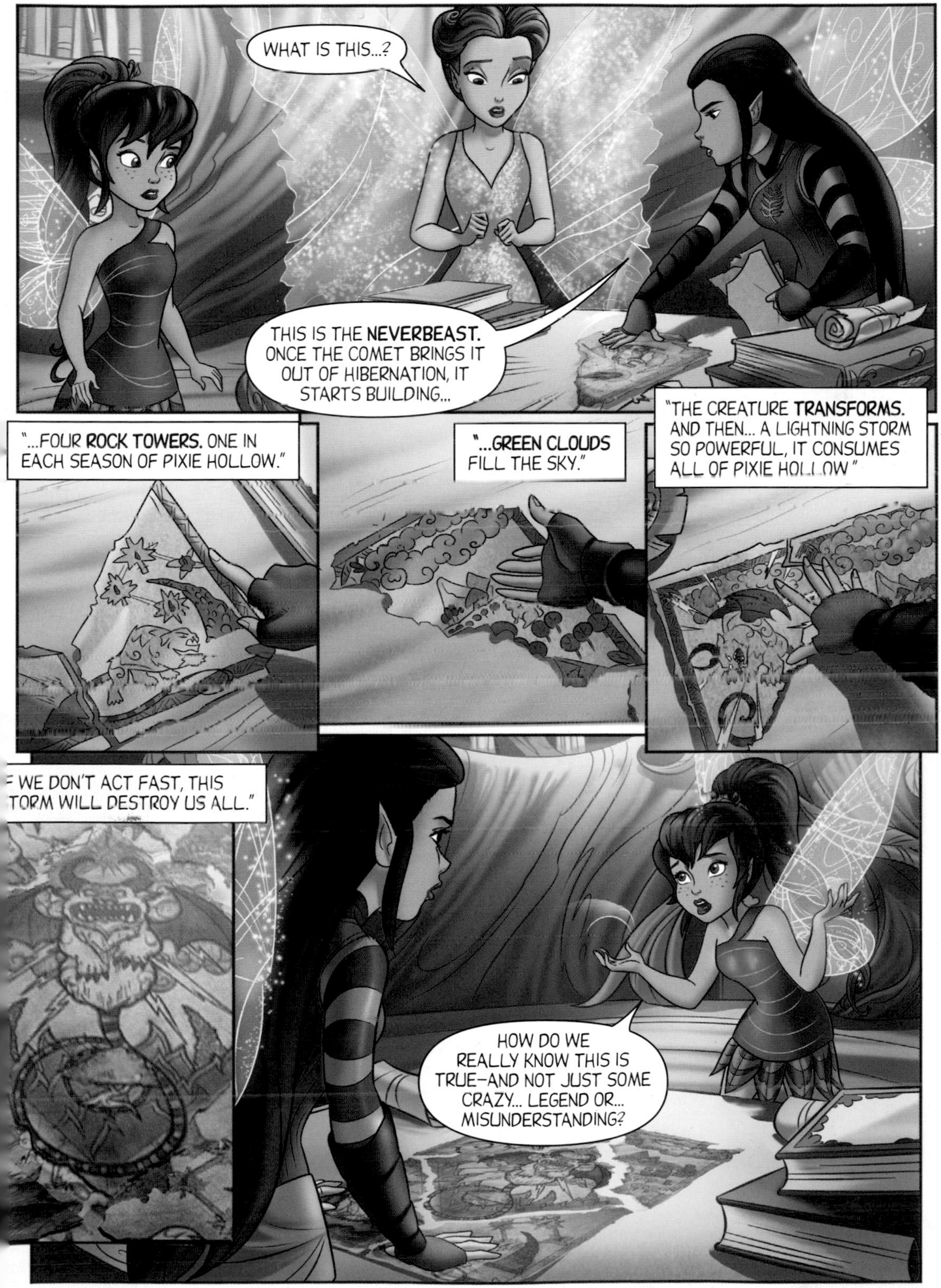
WHAT IS THIS...?
THIS IS THE NEVERBEAST. ONCE THE COMET BRINGS IT OUT OF HIBERNATION, IT STARTS BUILDING...
"...FOUR ROCK TOWERS. ONE IN EACH SEASON OF PIXIE HOLLOW."
"...GREEN CLOUDS FILL THE SKY."
"THE CREATURE TRANSFORMS. AND THEN... A LIGHTNING STORM SO POWERFUL, IT CONSUMES ALL OF PIXIE HOLLOW."
F WE DON'T ACT FAST, THIS TORM WILL DESTROY US ALL."
HOW DO WE REALLY KNOW THIS IS TRUE–AND NOT JUST SOME CRAZY... LEGEND OR... MISUNDERSTANDING?

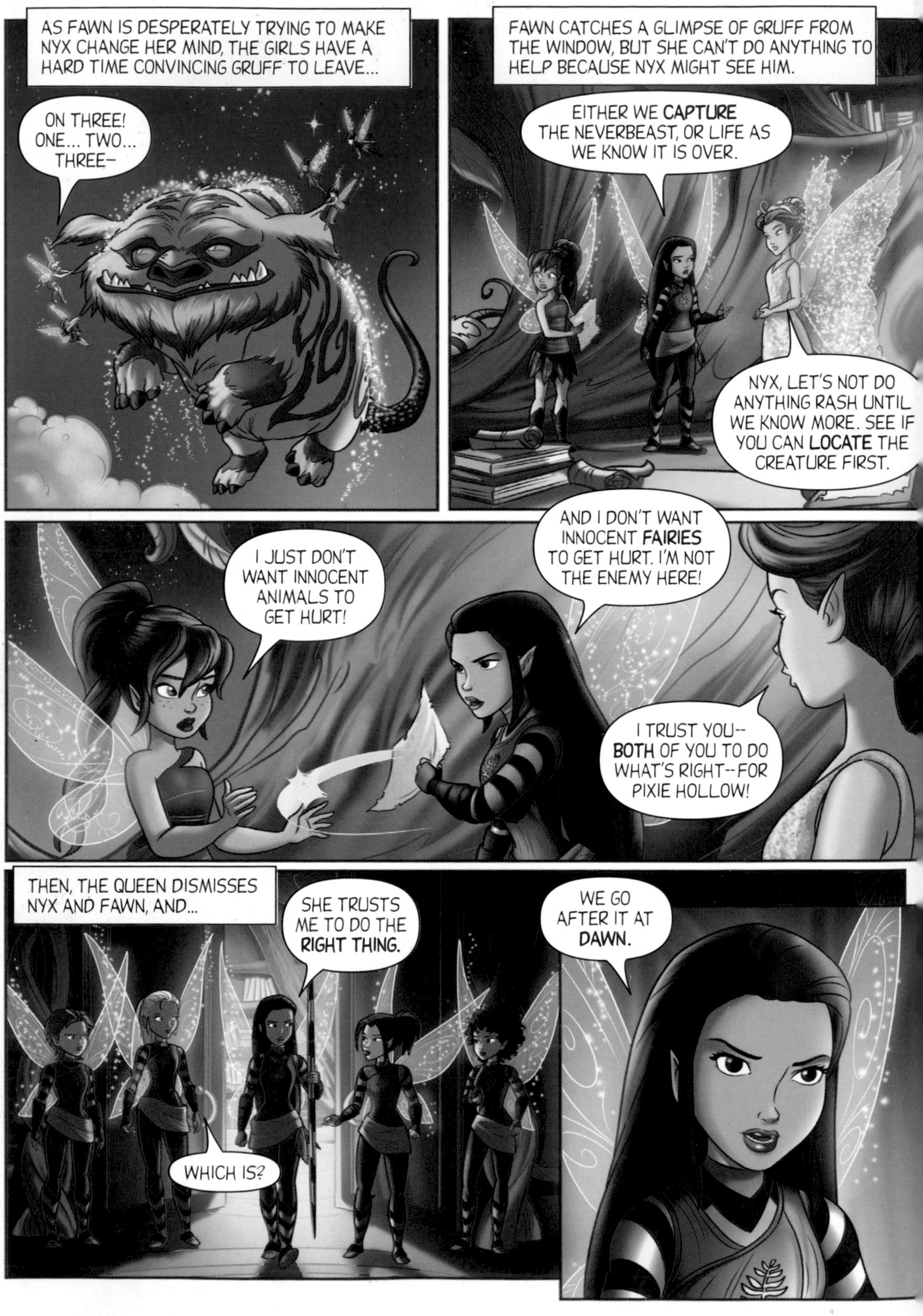
AS FAWN IS DESPERATELY TRYING TO MAKE NYX CHANGE HER MIND, THE GIRLS HAVE A HARD TIME CONVINCING GRUFF TO LEAVE...
ON THREE! ONE... TWO... THREE–
FAWN CATCHES A GLIMPSE OF GRUFF FROM THE WINDOW, BUT SHE CAN'T DO ANYTHING TO HELP BECAUSE NYX MIGHT SEE HIM.
EITHER WE **CAPTURE** THE NEVERBEAST, OR LIFE AS WE KNOW IT IS OVER.
NYX, LET'S NOT DO ANYTHING RASH UNTIL WE KNOW MORE. SEE IF YOU CAN **LOCATE** THE CREATURE FIRST.
I JUST DON'T WANT INNOCENT ANIMALS TO GET HURT!
AND I DON'T WANT INNOCENT **FAIRIES** TO GET HURT. I'M NOT THE ENEMY HERE!
I TRUST YOU-- **BOTH** OF YOU TO DO WHAT'S RIGHT--FOR PIXIE HOLLOW!
THEN, THE QUEEN DISMISSES NYX AND FAWN, AND...
SHE TRUSTS ME TO DO THE **RIGHT THING.**
WHICH IS?
WE GO AFTER IT AT **DAWN.**

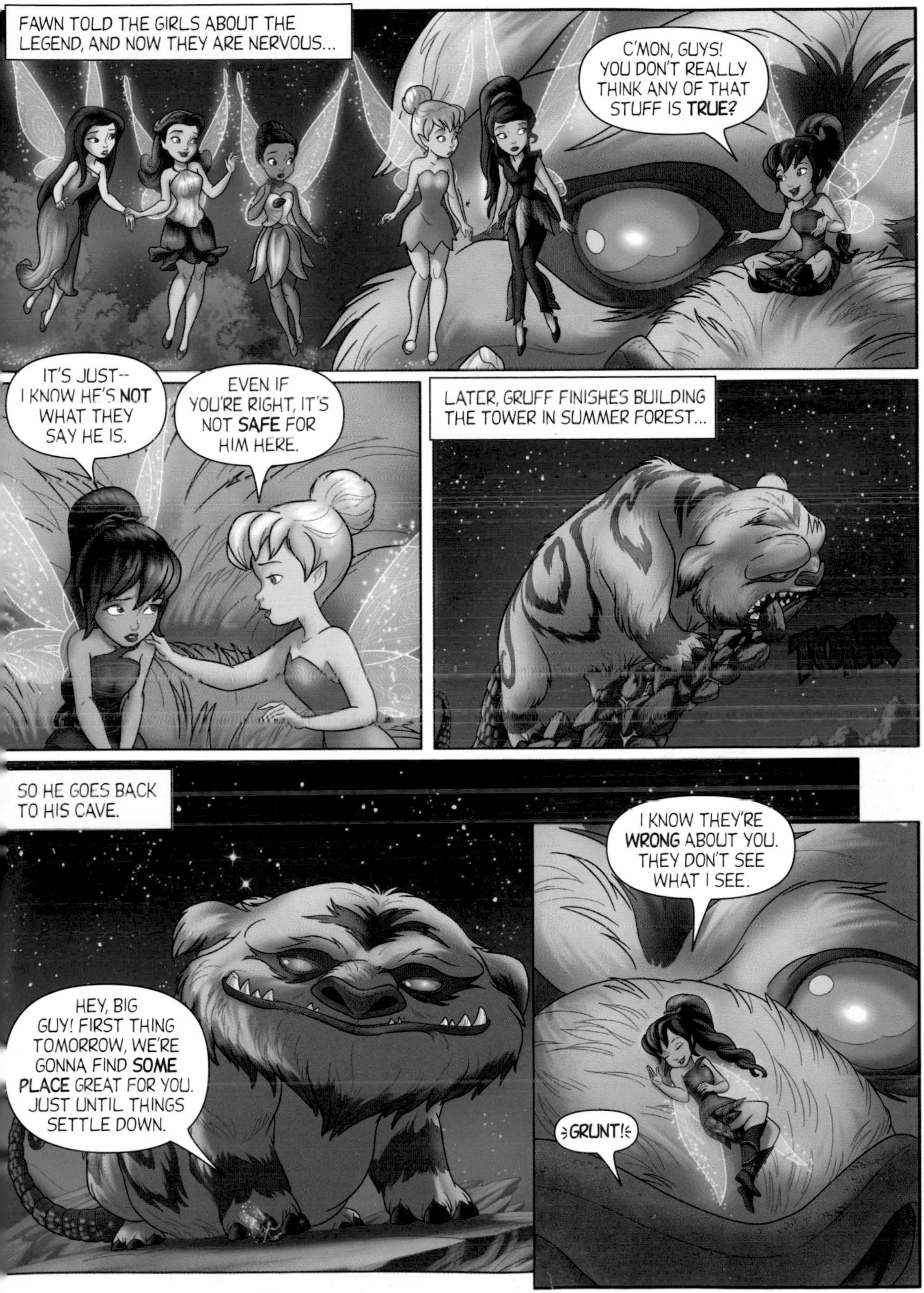
FAWN TOLD THE GIRLS ABOUT THE LEGEND, AND NOW THEY ARE NERVOUS...
C'MON, GUYS! YOU DON'T REALLY THINK ANY OF THAT STUFF IS TRUE?
IT'S JUST-- I KNOW HE'S NOT WHAT THEY SAY HE IS.
EVEN IF YOU'RE RIGHT, IT'S NOT SAFE FOR HIM HERE.
LATER, GRUFF FINISHES BUILDING THE TOWER IN SUMMER FOREST...
SO HE GOES BACK TO HIS CAVE.
HEY, BIG GUY! FIRST THING TOMORROW, WE'RE GONNA FIND SOME PLACE GREAT FOR YOU. JUST UNTIL THINGS SETTLE DOWN.
I KNOW THEY'RE WRONG ABOUT YOU. THEY DON'T SEE WHAT I SEE.
GRUNT!

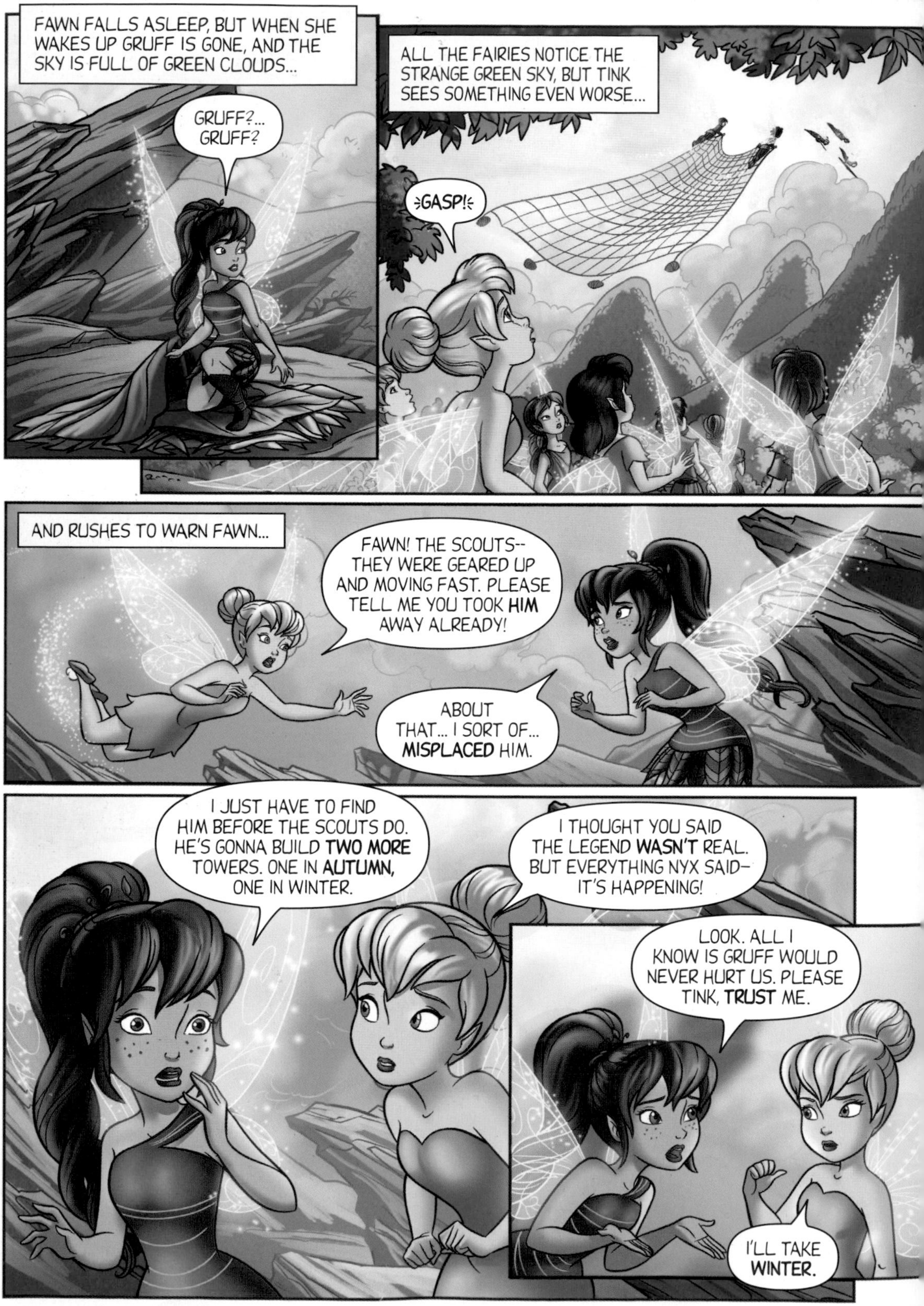
FAWN FALLS ASLEEP, BUT WHEN SHE WAKES UP GRUFF IS GONE, AND THE SKY IS FULL OF GREEN CLOUDS...
GRUFF?... GRUFF?
ALL THE FAIRIES NOTICE THE STRANGE GREEN SKY, BUT TINK SEES SOMETHING EVEN WORSE...
GASP!
AND RUSHES TO WARN FAWN...
FAWN! THE SCOUTS-- THEY WERE GEARED UP AND MOVING FAST. PLEASE TELL ME YOU TOOK HIM AWAY ALREADY!
ABOUT THAT... I SORT OF... MISPLACED HIM.
I JUST HAVE TO FIND HIM BEFORE THE SCOUTS DO. HE'S GONNA BUILD TWO MORE TOWERS. ONE IN AUTUMN, ONE IN WINTER.
I THOUGHT YOU SAID THE LEGEND WASN'T REAL. BUT EVERYTHING NYX SAID– IT'S HAPPENING!
LOOK. ALL I KNOW IS GRUFF WOULD NEVER HURT US. PLEASE TINK, TRUST ME.
I'LL TAKE WINTER.

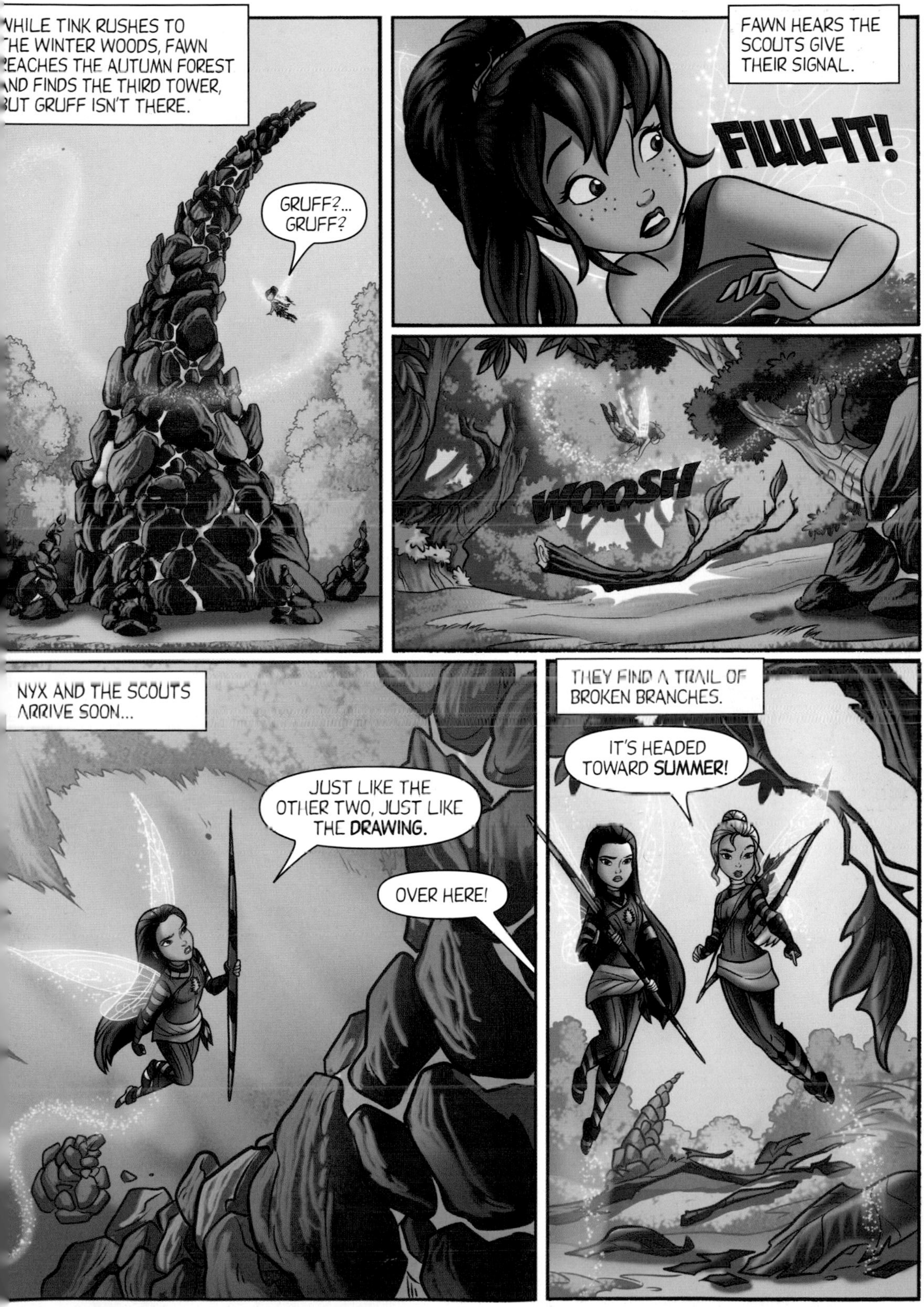

WHILE TINK RUSHES TO THE WINTER WOODS, FAWN REACHES THE AUTUMN FOREST AND FINDS THE THIRD TOWER, BUT GRUFF ISN'T THERE.
GRUFF?... GRUFF?
FAWN HEARS THE SCOUTS GIVE THEIR SIGNAL.
FIUU-IT!
WOOSH
NYX AND THE SCOUTS ARRIVE SOON...
JUST LIKE THE OTHER TWO, JUST LIKE THE **DRAWING**.
OVER HERE!
THEY FIND A TRAIL OF BROKEN BRANCHES.
IT'S HEADED TOWARD **SUMMER**!

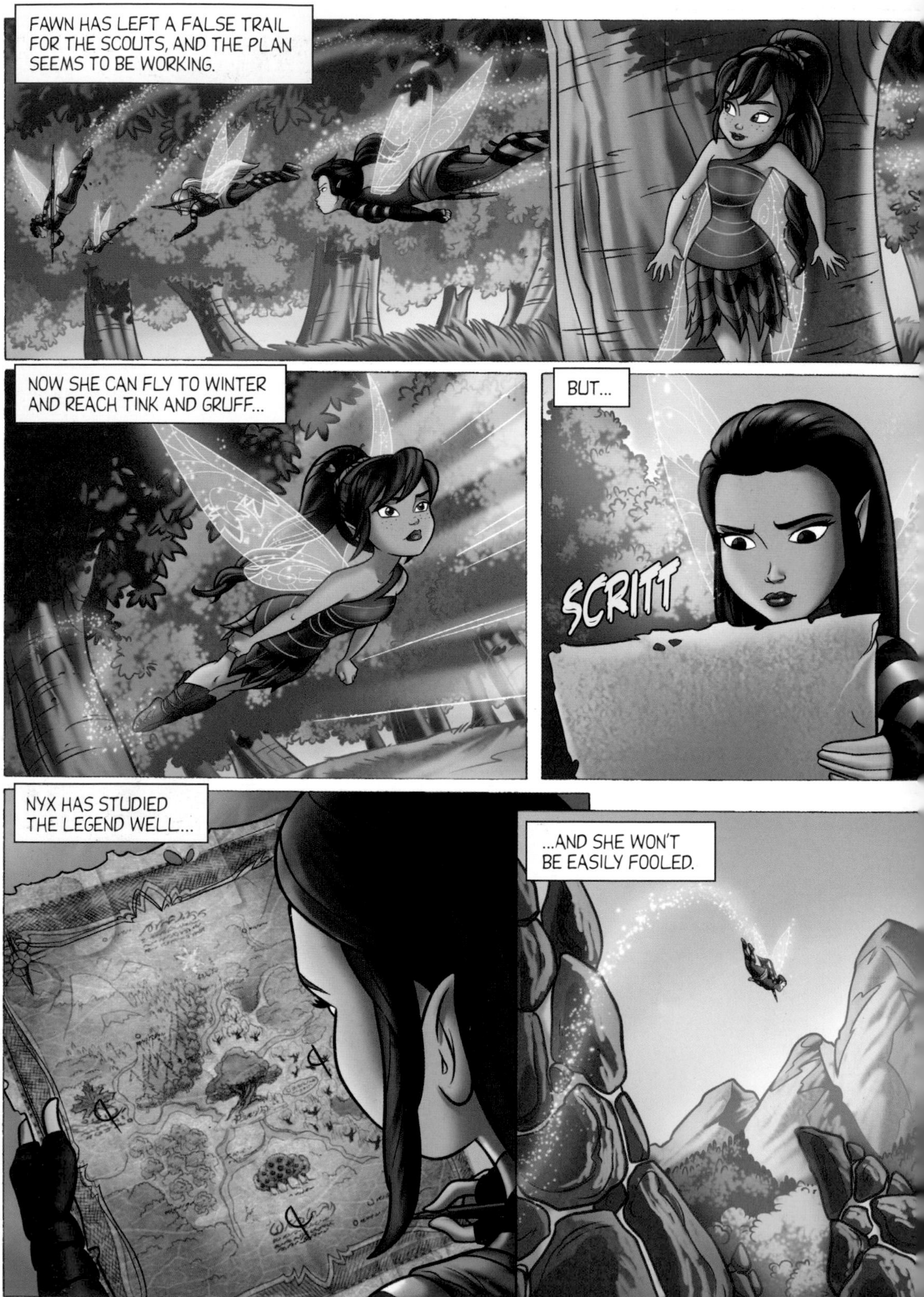
FAWN HAS LEFT A FALSE TRAIL FOR THE SCOUTS, AND THE PLAN SEEMS TO BE WORKING.
NOW SHE CAN FLY TO WINTER AND REACH TINK AND GRUFF...
BUT...
SCRITT
NYX HAS STUDIED THE LEGEND WELL...
...AND SHE WON'T BE EASILY FOOLED.

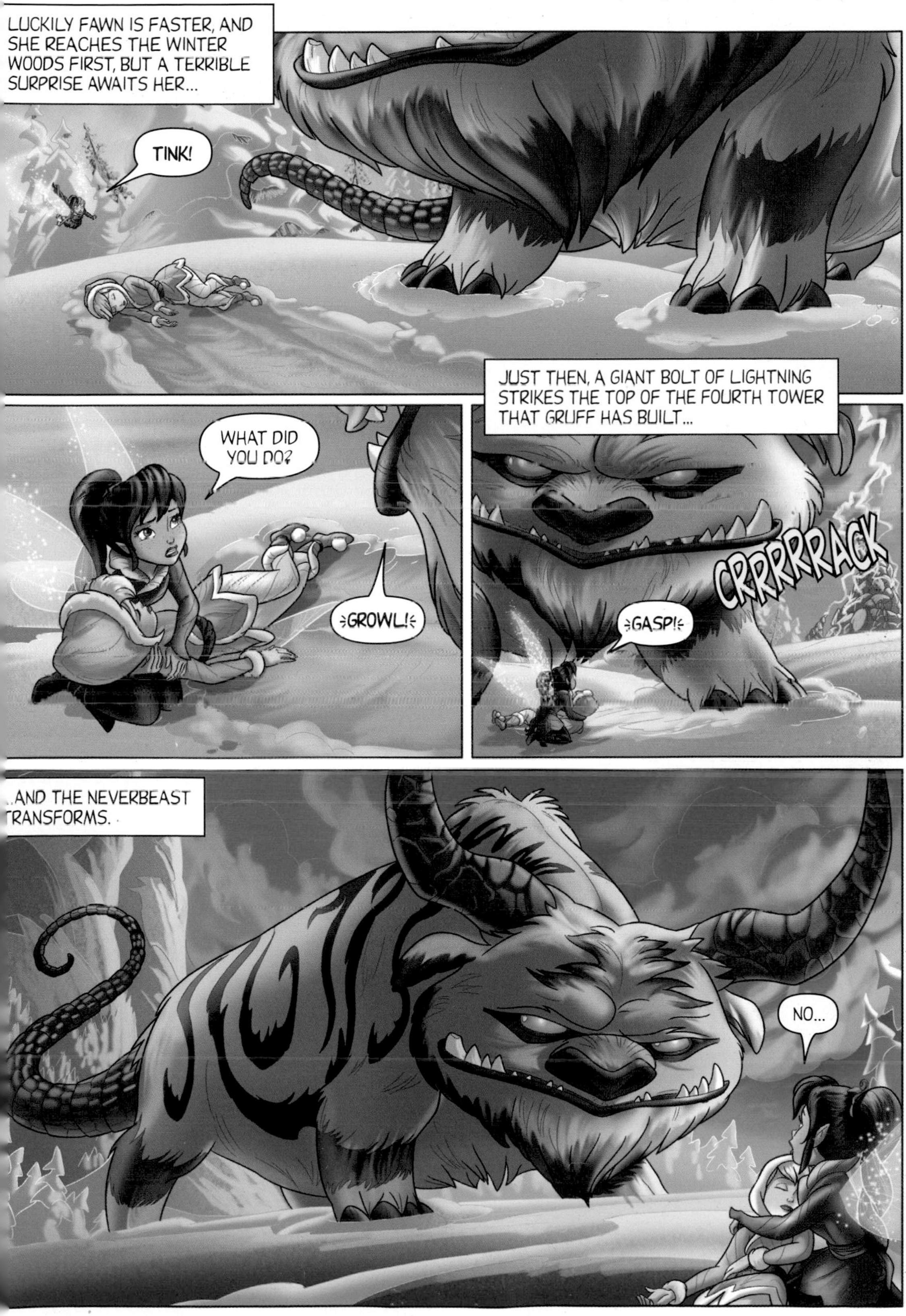

LUCKILY FAWN IS FASTER, AND SHE REACHES THE WINTER WOODS FIRST, BUT A TERRIBLE SURPRISE AWAITS HER...
TINK!
WHAT DID YOU DO?
GROWL!
JUST THEN, A GIANT BOLT OF LIGHTNING STRIKES THE TOP OF THE FOURTH TOWER THAT GRUFF HAS BUILT...
CRRRRRACK
GASP!
..AND THE NEVERBEAST TRANSFORMS.
NO...

PART FOUR:
"The Green Storm"

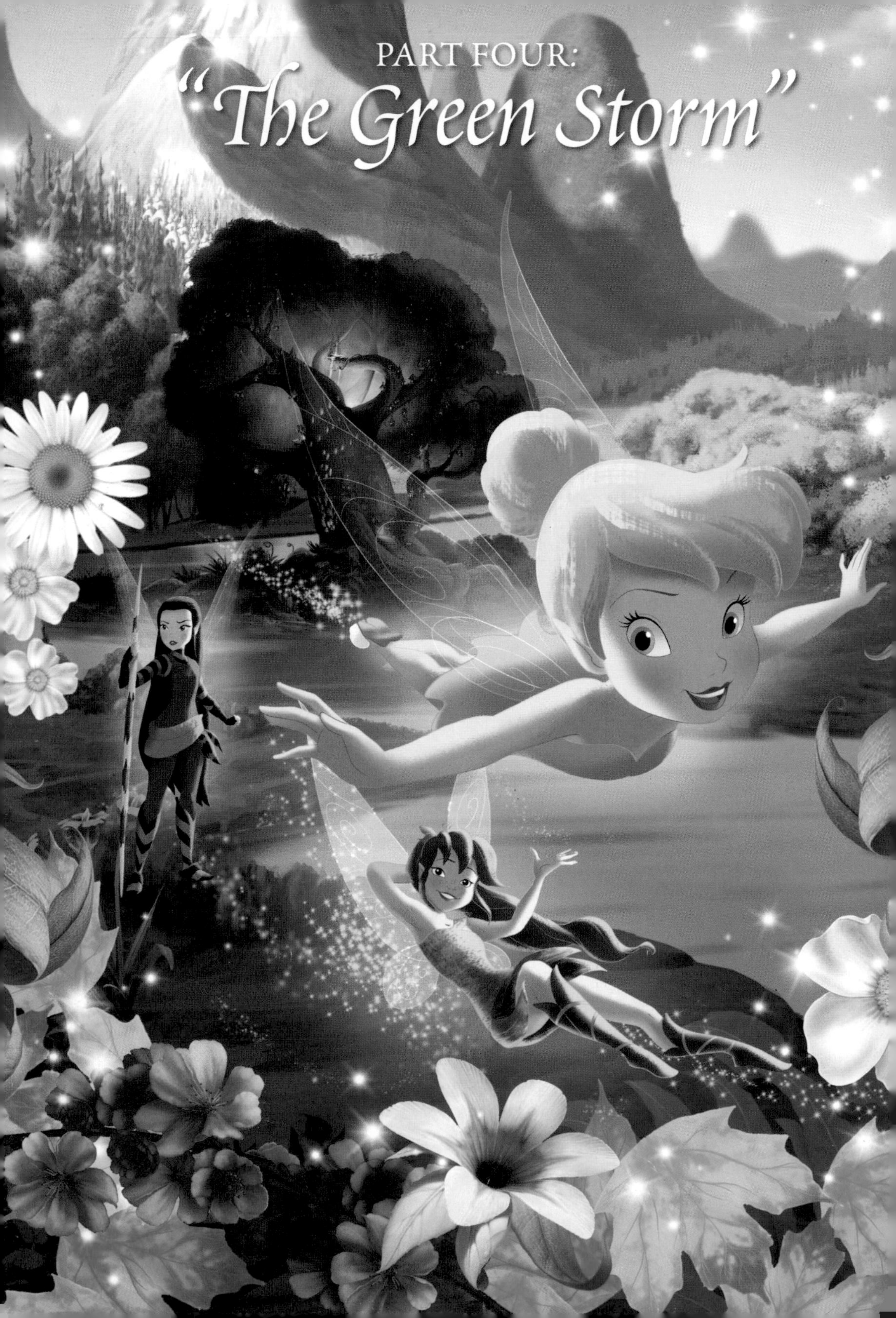

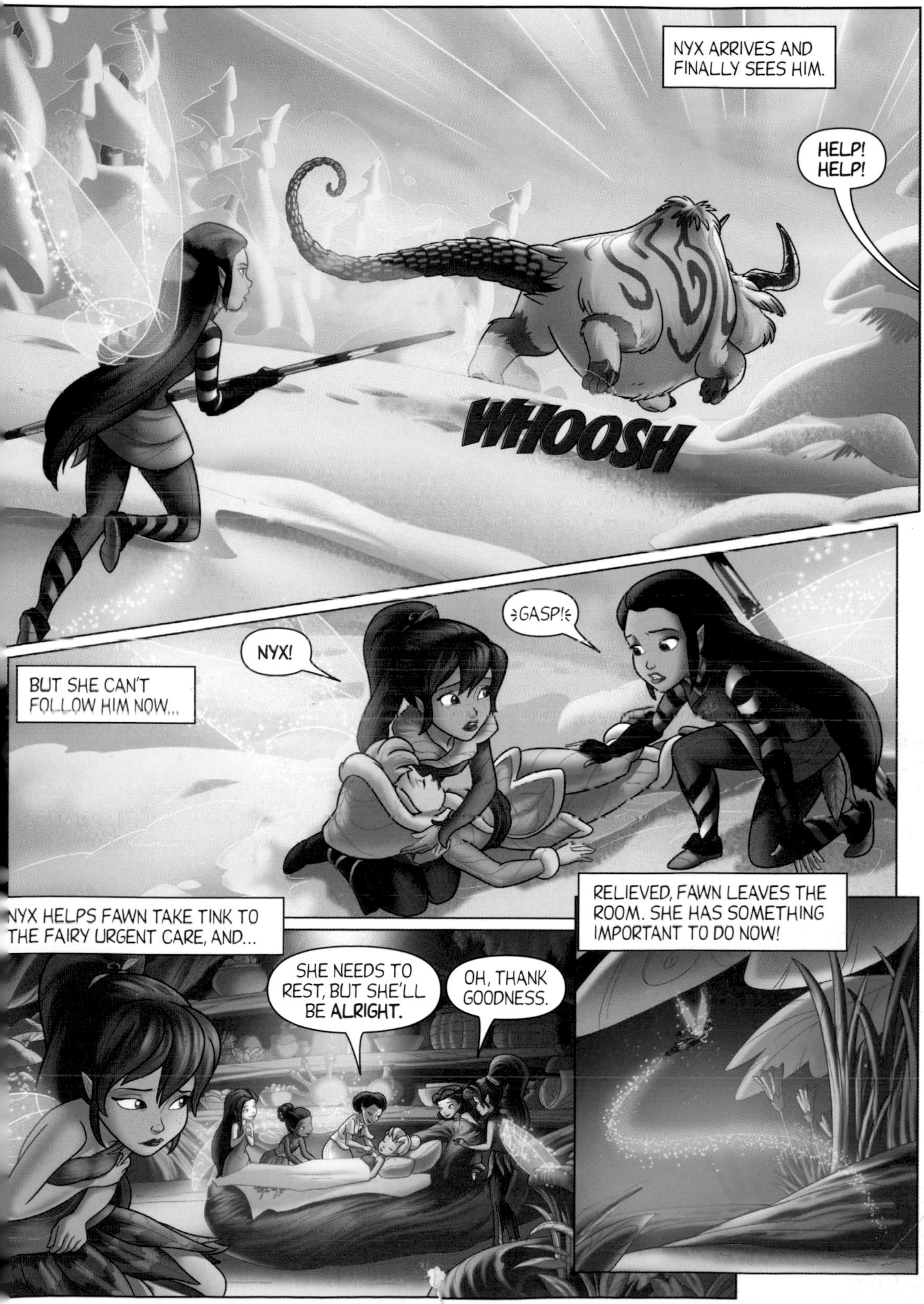

NYX ARRIVES AND FINALLY SEES HIM.
HELP! HELP!
WHOOSH
BUT SHE CAN'T FOLLOW HIM NOW...
NYX!
GASP!
NYX HELPS FAWN TAKE TINK TO THE FAIRY URGENT CARE, AND...
SHE NEEDS TO REST, BUT SHE'LL BE **ALRIGHT.**
OH, THANK GOODNESS.
RELIEVED, FAWN LEAVES THE ROOM. SHE HAS SOMETHING IMPORTANT TO DO NOW!

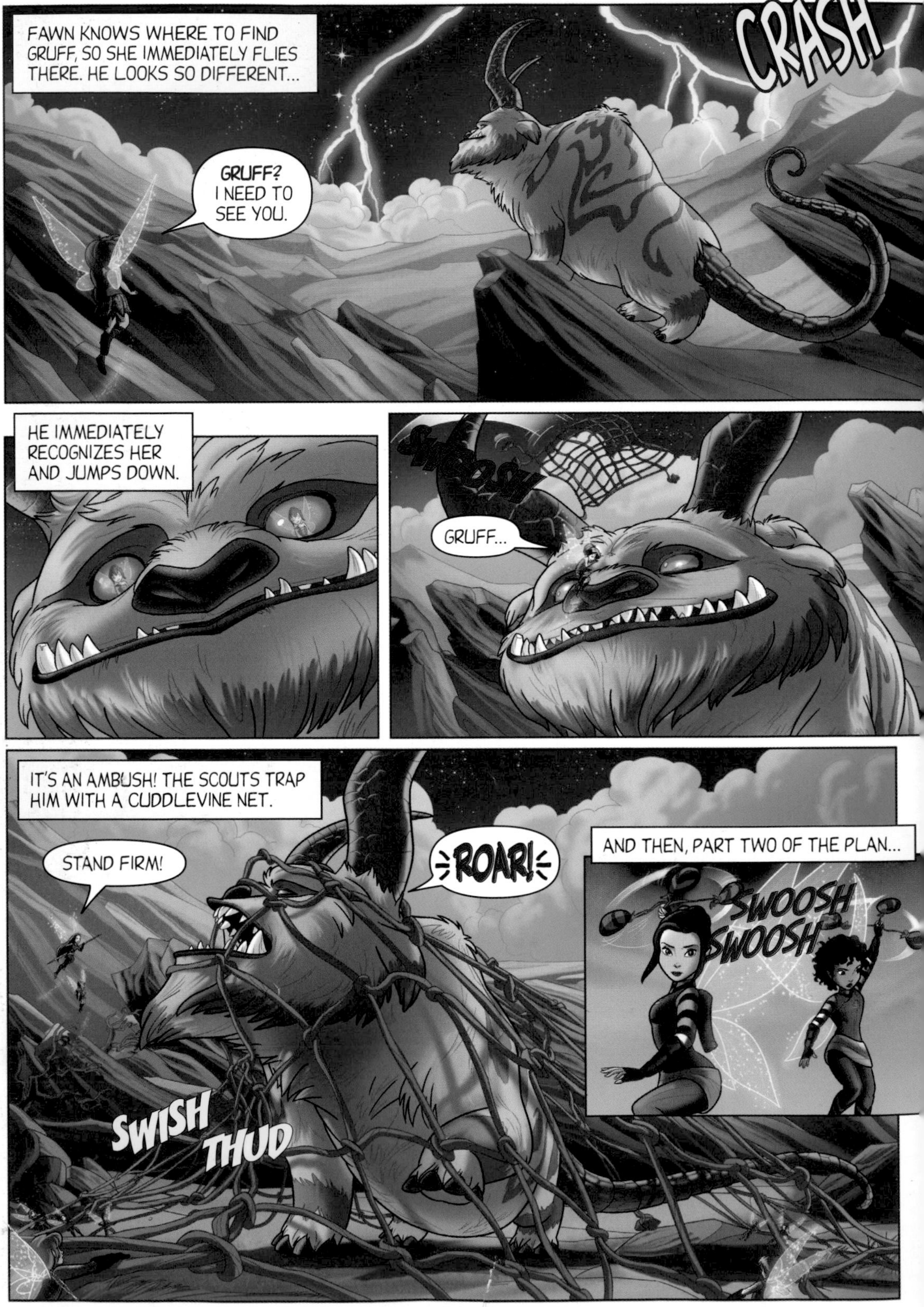
FAWN KNOWS WHERE TO FIND GRUFF, SO SHE IMMEDIATELY FLIES THERE. HE LOOKS SO DIFFERENT...
CRASH
GRUFF? I NEED TO SEE YOU.
HE IMMEDIATELY RECOGNIZES HER AND JUMPS DOWN.
SWOOSH
GRUFF...
IT'S AN AMBUSH! THE SCOUTS TRAP HIM WITH A CUDDLEVINE NET.
STAND FIRM!
ROAR!
SWISH
THUD
AND THEN, PART TWO OF THE PLAN...
SWOOSH
SWOOSH

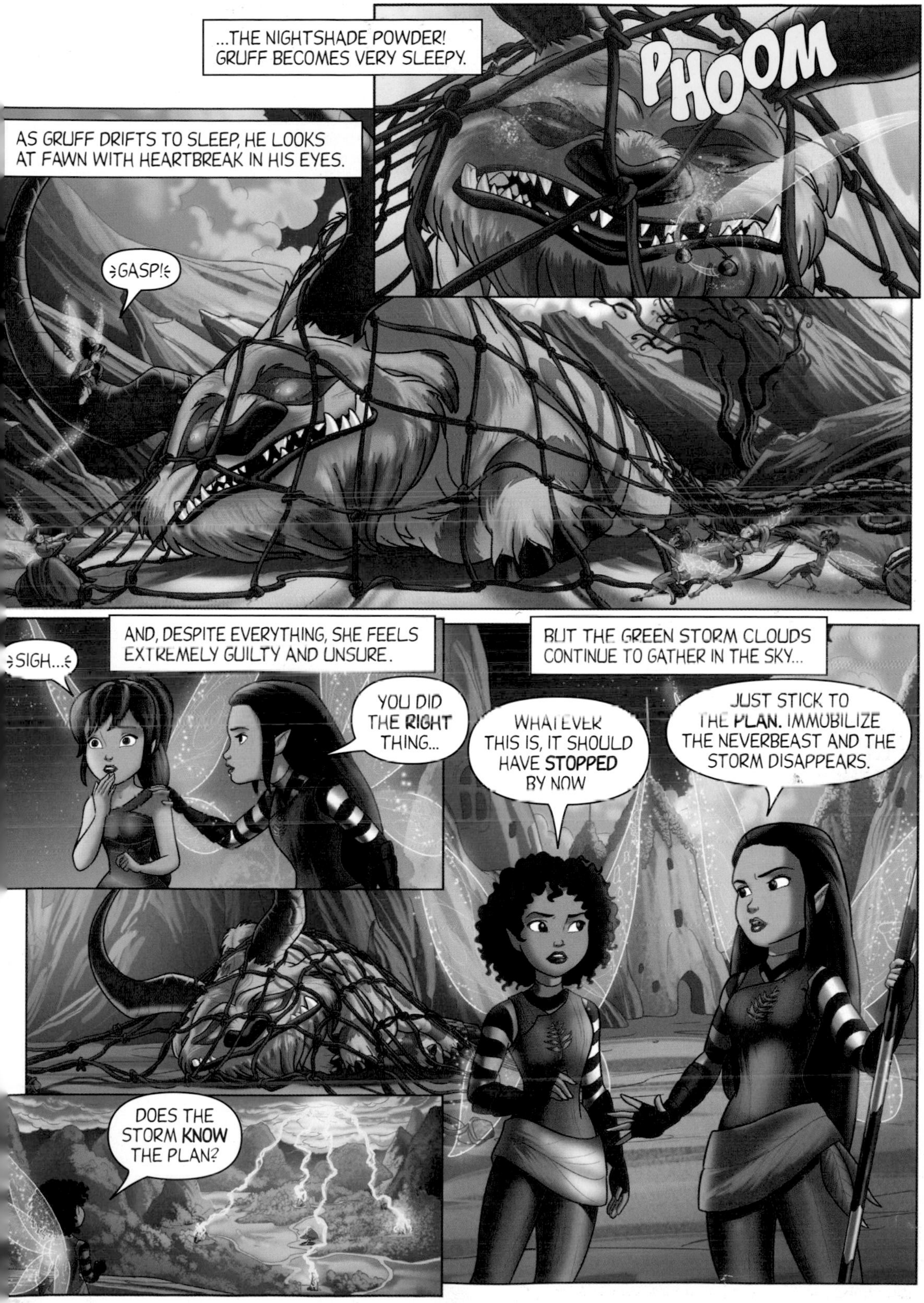
...THE NIGHTSHADE POWDER! GRUFF BECOMES VERY SLEEPY.
PHOOM
AS GRUFF DRIFTS TO SLEEP, HE LOOKS AT FAWN WITH HEARTBREAK IN HIS EYES.
GASP!
AND, DESPITE EVERYTHING, SHE FEELS EXTREMELY GUILTY AND UNSURE.
SIGH...
YOU DID THE **RIGHT** THING...
BUT THE GREEN STORM CLOUDS CONTINUE TO GATHER IN THE SKY...
WHATEVER THIS IS, IT SHOULD HAVE **STOPPED** BY NOW
JUST STICK TO THE **PLAN.** IMMOBILIZE THE NEVERBEAST AND THE STORM DISAPPEARS.
DOES THE STORM **KNOW** THE PLAN?

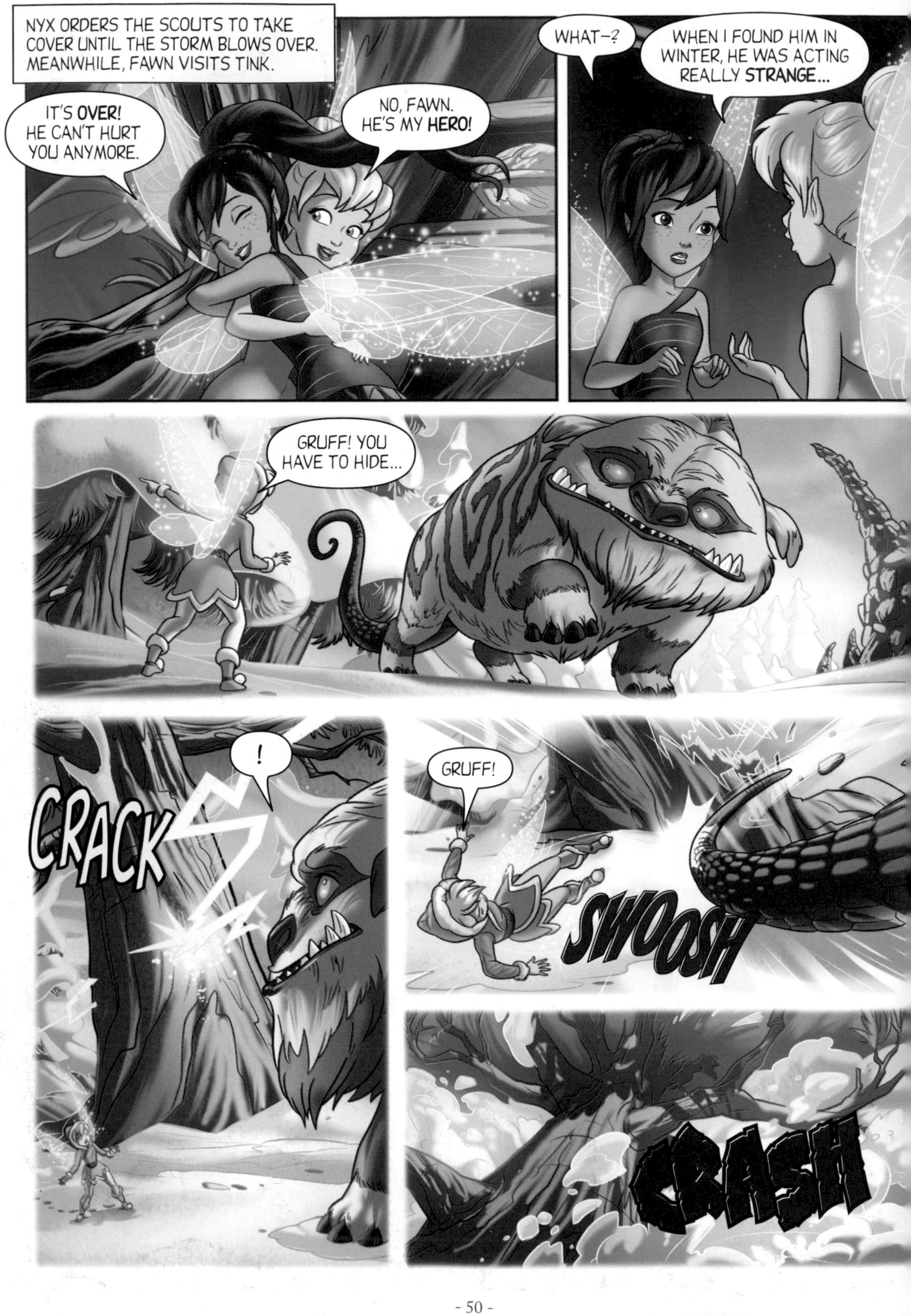
NYX ORDERS THE SCOUTS TO TAKE COVER UNTIL THE STORM BLOWS OVER. MEANWHILE, FAWN VISITS TINK.
IT'S **OVER!** HE CAN'T HURT YOU ANYMORE.
NO, FAWN. HE'S MY **HERO!**
WHAT–?
WHEN I FOUND HIM IN WINTER, HE WAS ACTING REALLY **STRANGE...**
GRUFF! YOU HAVE TO HIDE...
CRACK
!
GRUFF!
SWOOSH
CRASH

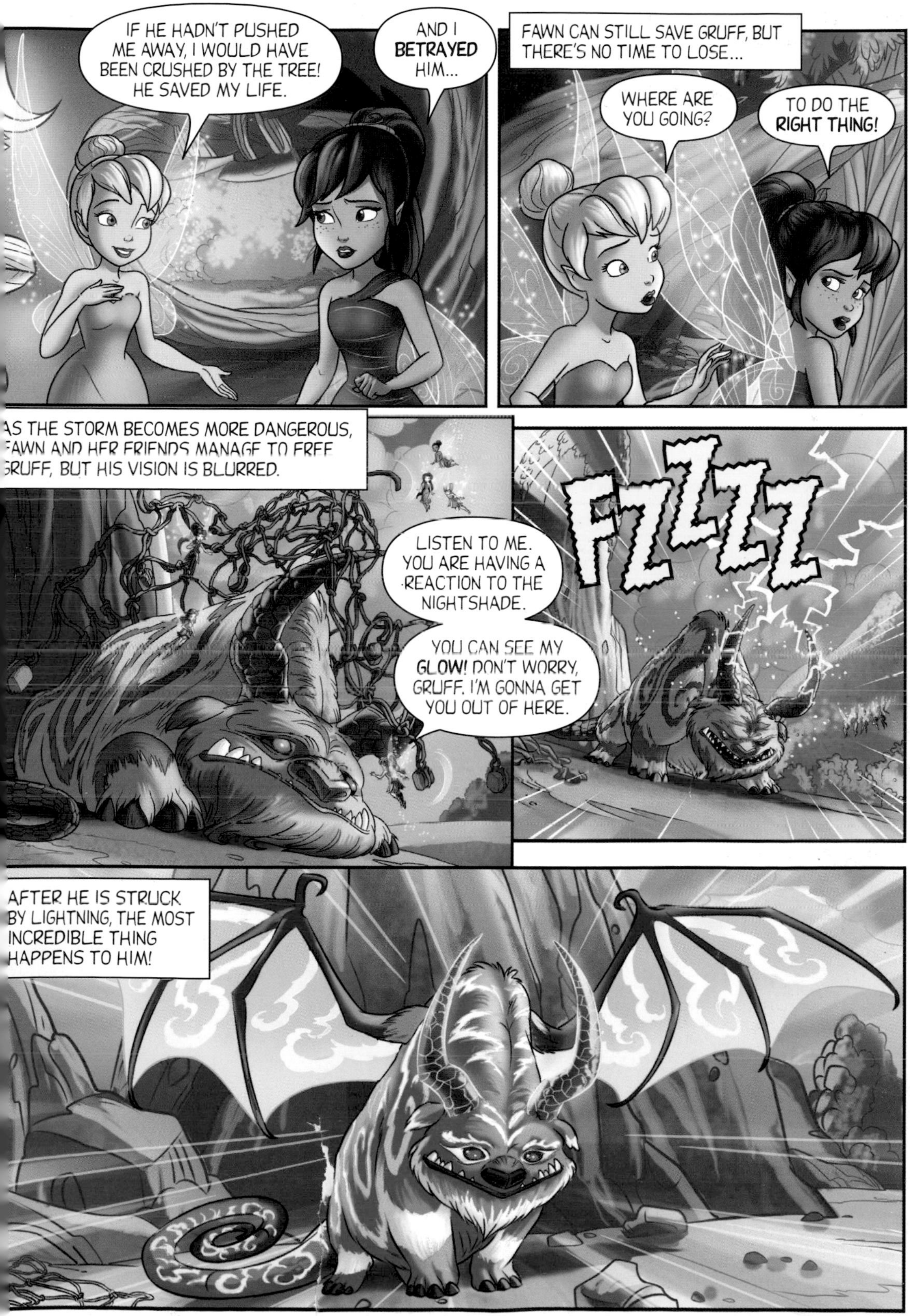
IF HE HADN'T PUSHED ME AWAY, I WOULD HAVE BEEN CRUSHED BY THE TREE! HE SAVED MY LIFE.
AND I BETRAYED HIM...
FAWN CAN STILL SAVE GRUFF, BUT THERE'S NO TIME TO LOSE...
WHERE ARE YOU GOING?
TO DO THE RIGHT THING!
AS THE STORM BECOMES MORE DANGEROUS, FAWN AND HER FRIENDS MANAGE TO FREE GRUFF, BUT HIS VISION IS BLURRED.
LISTEN TO ME. YOU ARE HAVING A REACTION TO THE NIGHTSHADE.
YOU CAN SEE MY GLOW! DON'T WORRY, GRUFF. I'M GONNA GET YOU OUT OF HERE.
FZZZZ
AFTER HE IS STRUCK BY LIGHTNING, THE MOST INCREDIBLE THING HAPPENS TO HIM!

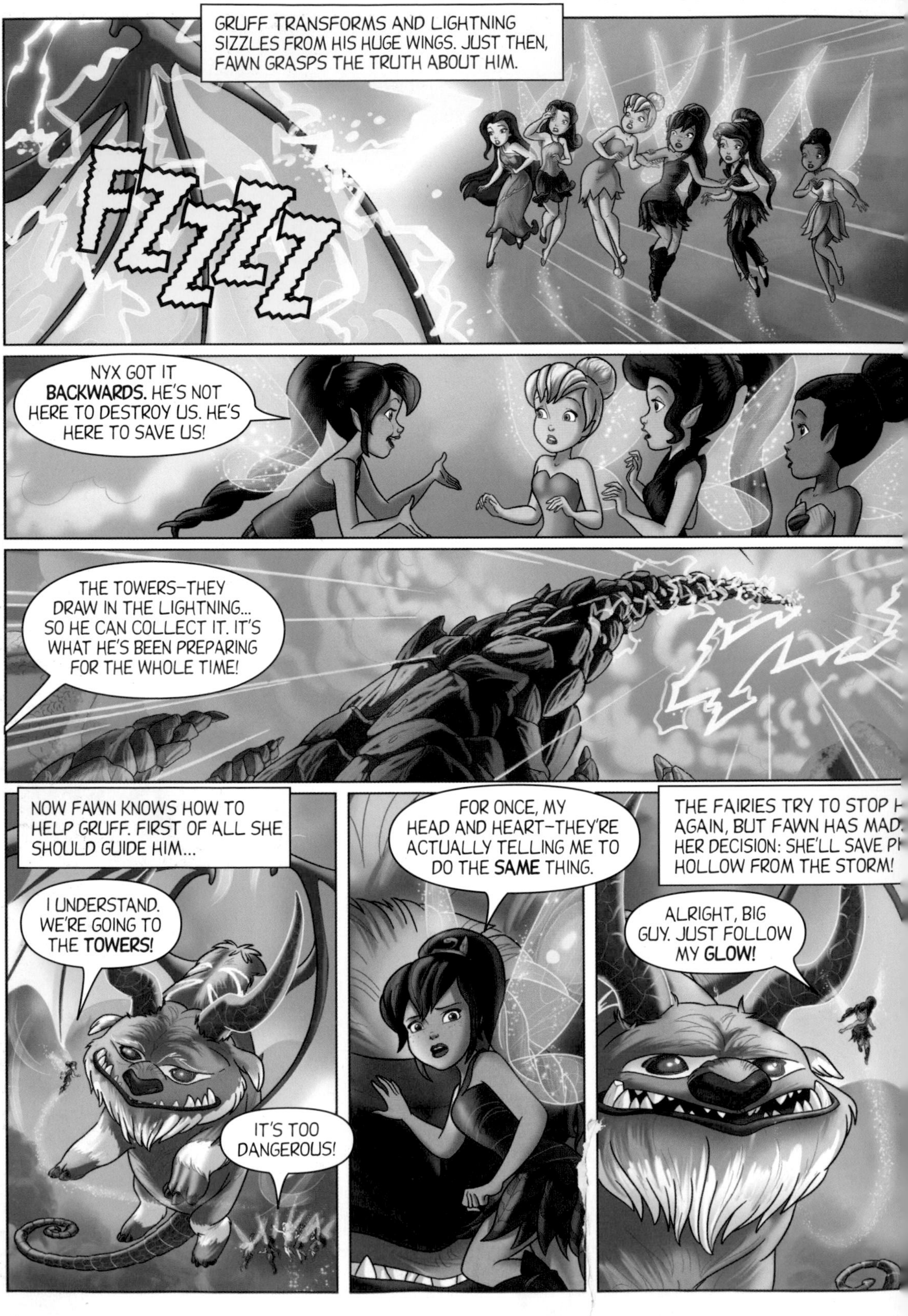
GRUFF TRANSFORMS AND LIGHTNING SIZZLES FROM HIS HUGE WINGS. JUST THEN, FAWN GRASPS THE TRUTH ABOUT HIM.
FZZZZ
NYX GOT IT **BACKWARDS.** HE'S NOT HERE TO DESTROY US. HE'S HERE TO SAVE US!
THE TOWERS—THEY DRAW IN THE LIGHTNING... SO HE CAN COLLECT IT. IT'S WHAT HE'S BEEN PREPARING FOR THE WHOLE TIME!
NOW FAWN KNOWS HOW TO HELP GRUFF. FIRST OF ALL SHE SHOULD GUIDE HIM...
I UNDERSTAND. WE'RE GOING TO THE **TOWERS!**
IT'S TOO DANGEROUS!
FOR ONCE, MY HEAD AND HEART—THEY'RE ACTUALLY TELLING ME TO DO THE **SAME** THING.
THE FAIRIES TRY TO STOP H AGAIN, BUT FAWN HAS MAD HER DECISION: SHE'LL SAVE PI HOLLOW FROM THE STORM!
ALRIGHT, BIG GUY. JUST FOLLOW MY **GLOW!**

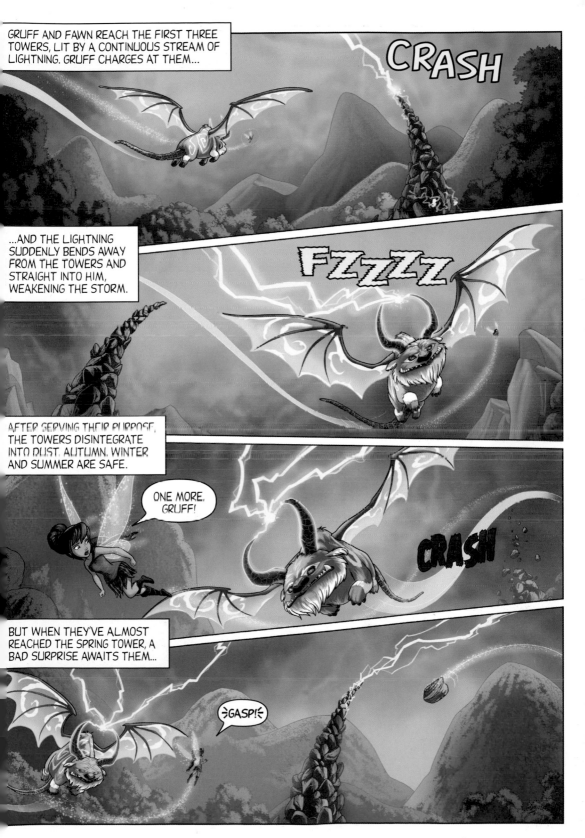

GRUFF AND FAWN REACH THE FIRST THREE TOWERS, LIT BY A CONTINUOUS STREAM OF LIGHTNING. GRUFF CHARGES AT THEM...

CRASH

...AND THE LIGHTNING SUDDENLY BENDS AWAY FROM THE TOWERS AND STRAIGHT INTO HIM, WEAKENING THE STORM.

FZZZZZ

AFTER SERVING THEIR PURPOSE, THE TOWERS DISINTEGRATE INTO DUST. AUTUMN, WINTER AND SUMMER ARE SAFE.

ONE MORE, GRUFF!

CRASH

BUT WHEN THEY'VE ALMOST REACHED THE SPRING TOWER, A BAD SURPRISE AWAITS THEM...

≷GASP!≷

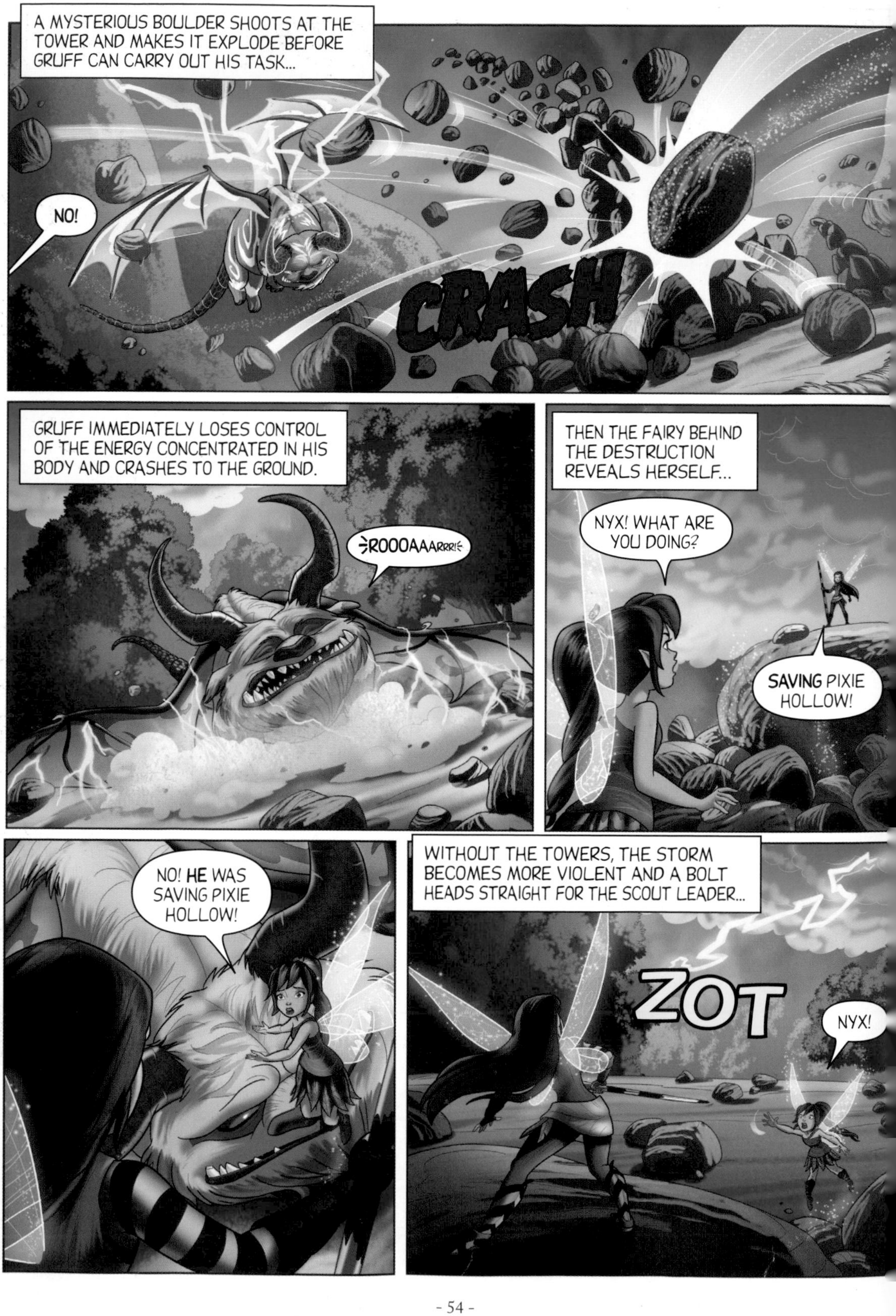

A MYSTERIOUS BOULDER SHOOTS AT THE TOWER AND MAKES IT EXPLODE BEFORE GRUFF CAN CARRY OUT HIS TASK...
NO!
CRASH
GRUFF IMMEDIATELY LOSES CONTROL OF THE ENERGY CONCENTRATED IN HIS BODY AND CRASHES TO THE GROUND.
ROOOAAARRR!
THEN THE FAIRY BEHIND THE DESTRUCTION REVEALS HERSELF...
NYX! WHAT ARE YOU DOING?
SAVING PIXIE HOLLOW!
NO! HE WAS SAVING PIXIE HOLLOW!
WITHOUT THE TOWERS, THE STORM BECOMES MORE VIOLENT AND A BOLT HEADS STRAIGHT FOR THE SCOUT LEADER...
ZOT
NYX!

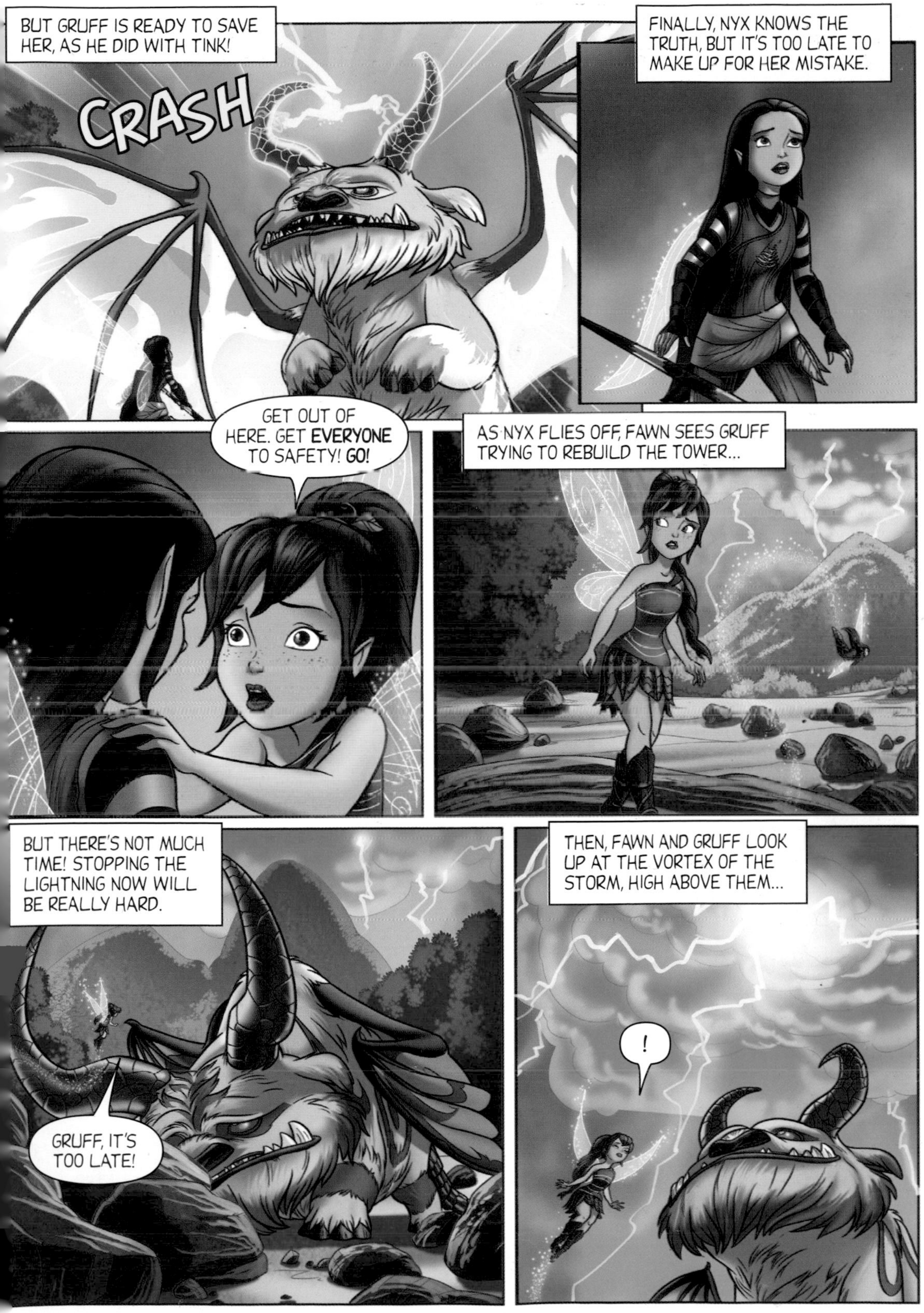
BUT GRUFF IS READY TO SAVE HER, AS HE DID WITH TINK!
CRASH
FINALLY, NYX KNOWS THE TRUTH, BUT IT'S TOO LATE TO MAKE UP FOR HER MISTAKE.
GET OUT OF HERE. GET **EVERYONE** TO SAFETY! **GO!**
AS NYX FLIES OFF, FAWN SEES GRUFF TRYING TO REBUILD THE TOWER...
BUT THERE'S NOT MUCH TIME! STOPPING THE LIGHTNING NOW WILL BE REALLY HARD.
GRUFF, IT'S TOO LATE!
THEN, FAWN AND GRUFF LOOK UP AT THE VORTEX OF THE STORM, HIGH ABOVE THEM...
!

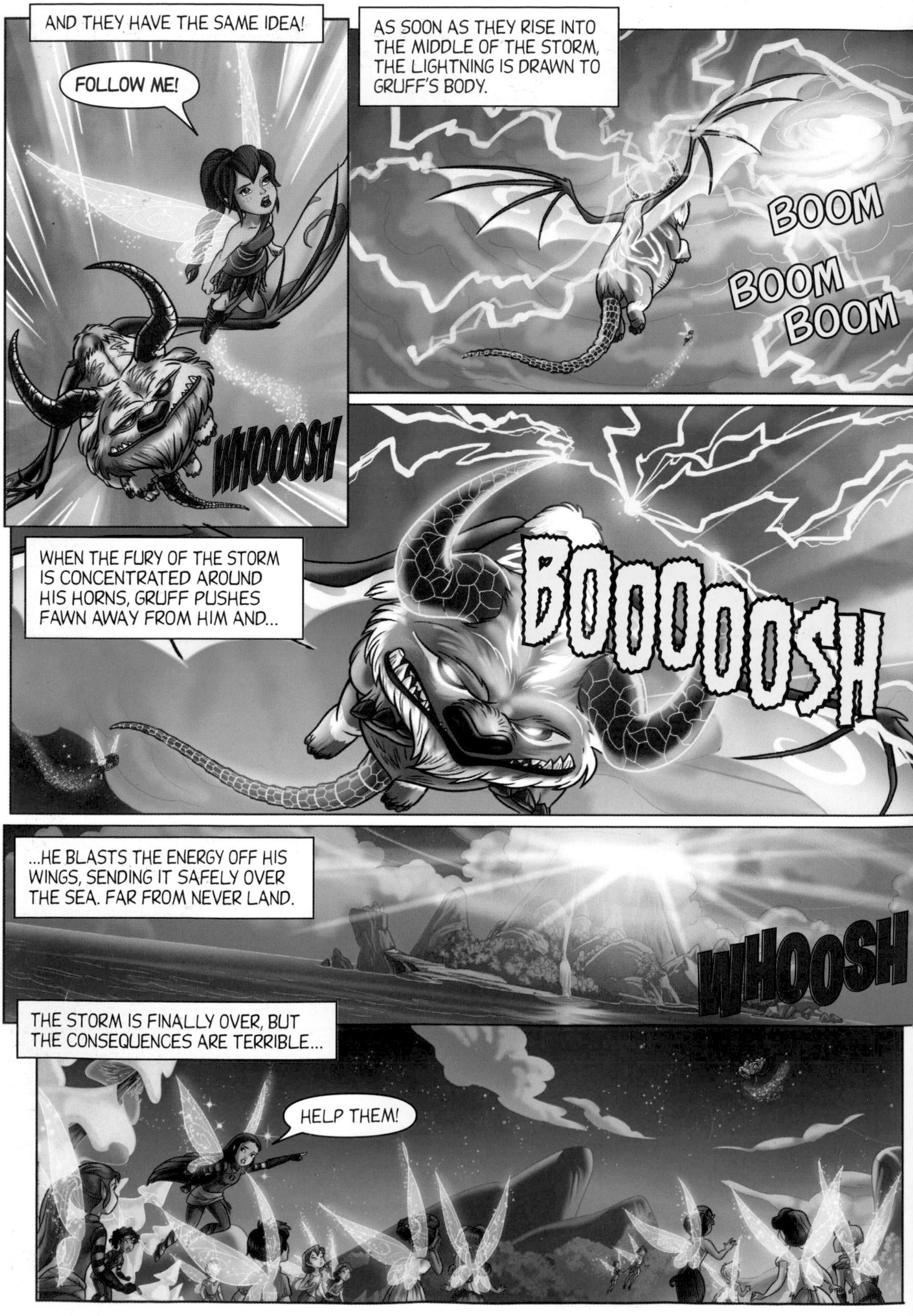
AND THEY HAVE THE SAME IDEA!
FOLLOW ME!
WHOOOSH
AS SOON AS THEY RISE INTO THE MIDDLE OF THE STORM, THE LIGHTNING IS DRAWN TO GRUFF'S BODY.
BOOM
BOOM
BOOM
WHEN THE FURY OF THE STORM IS CONCENTRATED AROUND HIS HORNS, GRUFF PUSHES FAWN AWAY FROM HIM AND...
BOOOOOOSH
...HE BLASTS THE ENERGY OFF HIS WINGS, SENDING IT SAFELY OVER THE SEA. FAR FROM NEVER LAND.
WHOOSH
THE STORM IS FINALLY OVER, BUT THE CONSEQUENCES ARE TERRIBLE...
HELP THEM!

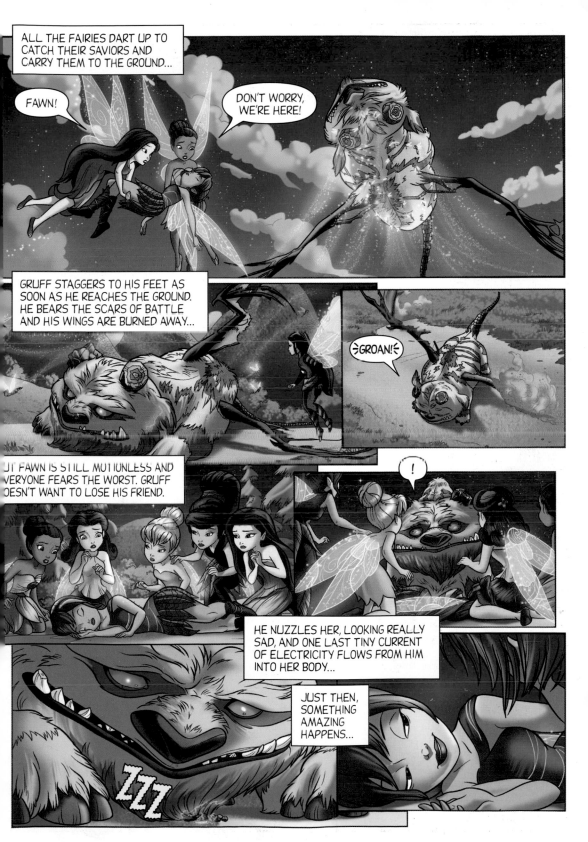

ALL THE FAIRIES DART UP TO CATCH THEIR SAVIORS AND CARRY THEM TO THE GROUND...

FAWN!

DON'T WORRY, WE'RE HERE!

GRUFF STAGGERS TO HIS FEET AS SOON AS HE REACHES THE GROUND. HE BEARS THE SCARS OF BATTLE AND HIS WINGS ARE BURNED AWAY...

GROAN!

UT FAWN IS STILL MOTIONLESS AND EVERYONE FEARS THE WORST. GRUFF OESN'T WANT TO LOSE HIS FRIEND.

!

HE NUZZLES HER, LOOKING REALLY SAD, AND ONE LAST TINY CURRENT OF ELECTRICITY FLOWS FROM HIM INTO HER BODY...

JUST THEN, SOMETHING AMAZING HAPPENS...

ZZZ

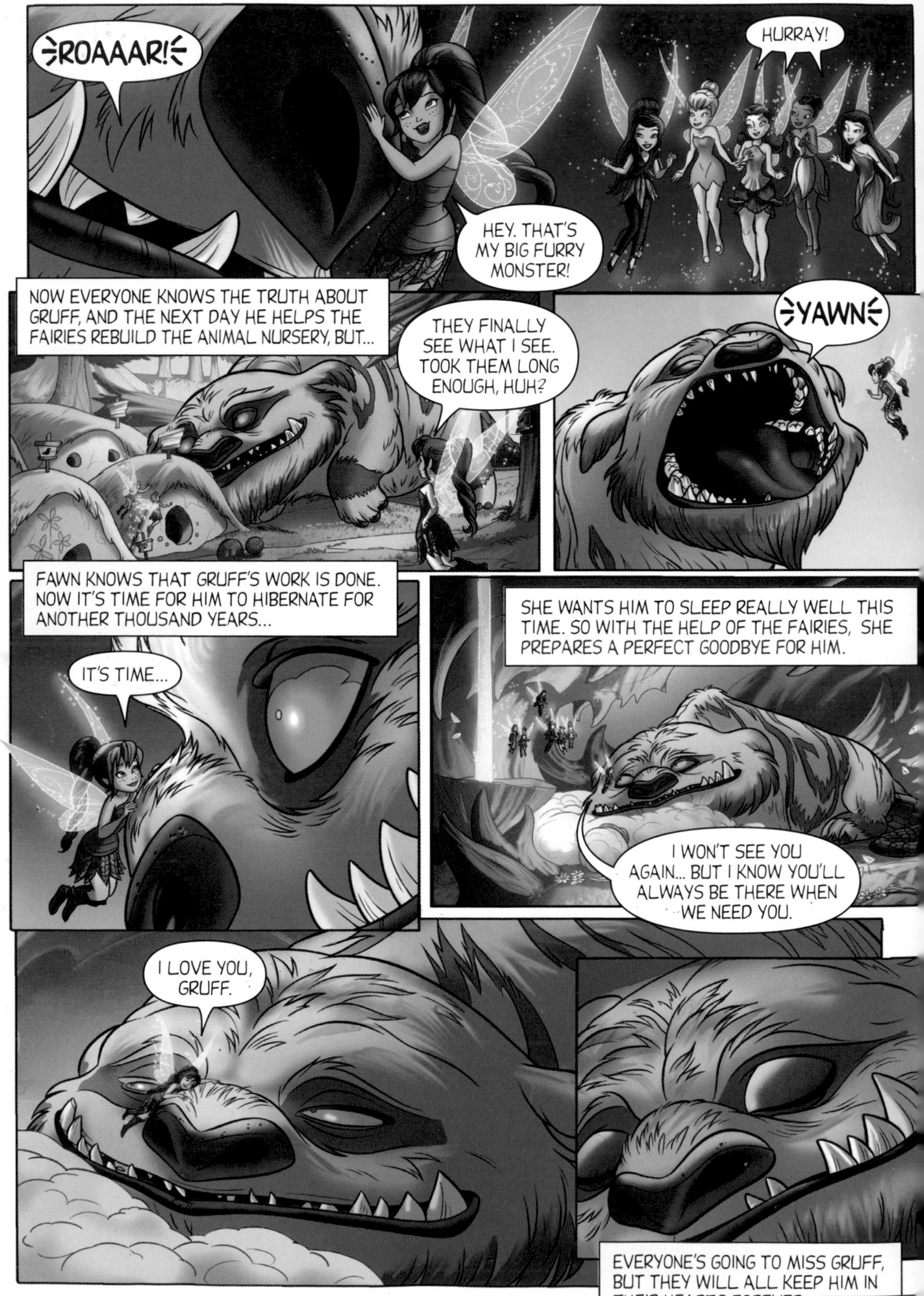

ROAAAR!
HEY. THAT'S MY BIG FURRY MONSTER!
HURRAY!
NOW EVERYONE KNOWS THE TRUTH ABOUT GRUFF, AND THE NEXT DAY HE HELPS THE FAIRIES REBUILD THE ANIMAL NURSERY, BUT...
THEY FINALLY SEE WHAT I SEE. TOOK THEM LONG ENOUGH, HUH?
YAWN
FAWN KNOWS THAT GRUFF'S WORK IS DONE. NOW IT'S TIME FOR HIM TO HIBERNATE FOR ANOTHER THOUSAND YEARS...
IT'S TIME...
SHE WANTS HIM TO SLEEP REALLY WELL THIS TIME. SO WITH THE HELP OF THE FAIRIES, SHE PREPARES A PERFECT GOODBYE FOR HIM.
I WON'T SEE YOU AGAIN... BUT I KNOW YOU'LL ALWAYS BE THERE WHEN WE NEED YOU.
I LOVE YOU, GRUFF.
EVERYONE'S GOING TO MISS GRUFF, BUT THEY WILL ALL KEEP HIM IN THEIR HEARTS FOREVER.
THE END.

WATCH OUT FOR PAPERCUTZ

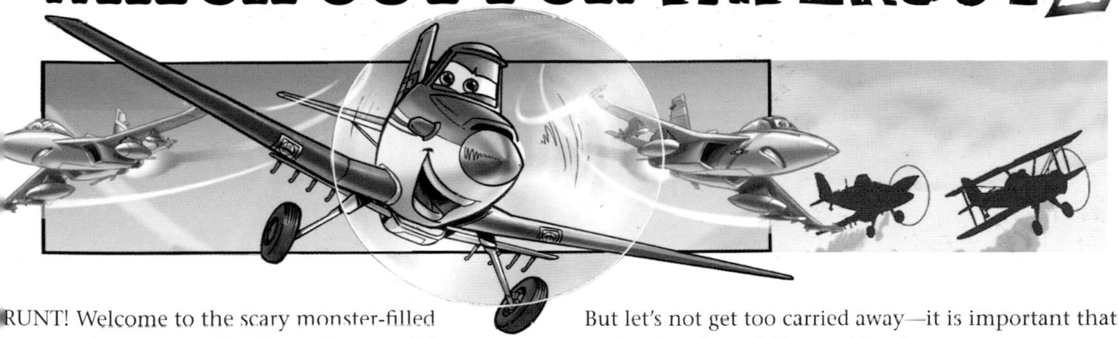

RUNT! Welcome to the scary monster-filled venteenth DISNEY FAIRIES graphic novel from ıpercutz, those daring dreamers dedicated to ıblishing great graphic novels for all ages. I'm Jim licrup, the Editor-in-Chief, and I'm here to reflect ›out fairies, NeverBeasts, and to correct a previous G ANNOUNCEMENT!

'inker Bell and the NeverBeast," like DISNEY FAIRIES 6 ""Tinker Bell and The Pirate Fairy," is truly a ought-provoking, while still highly entertaining, aphic novel. What do I mean by that? Well, when owing up we all tend to trust others to guide us ıd protect us while we struggle to figure out how to e in our world. For example, if parents or teachers l us not to do a certain thing, we listen because we ıow they love us and only have our best interests mind. But what happens when friends tell us to ware of something that we truly feel is not a danger us at all? Like when Fawn befriends the NeverBeast, e's certainly aware there's a certain amount of risk volved. As an animal-talent fairy she knows that most any animal could pose a potential threat, but r special talent and experience have given her an ıderstanding of certain creatures that others may not ve. And it's because of her believing in the goodness all creatures great and small, that she doesn't listen the well-intentioned advice of others. Now this esn't mean that Nyx is a villain. Not at all! She was ways doing what she truly believed was best to keep of the fairies in Pixie Hollow, including Fawn, as safe possible. Sometimes though, even when we have the ry best intentions, we could be wrong, as Nyx was.

But let's not get too carried away—it is important that we heed and carefully consider the warnings we get from others, especially from our families and friends. It's always better to be safe than sorry.

Also, in the "Watch Out for Papercutz" page in DISNEY FAIRIES #16, I made a BIG ANNOUNCEMENT that Papercutz would soon be publishing one of the longest running comicbooks as a graphic novel series. I was talking about WALT DISNEY'S COMICS AND STORIES, a series that has already run over 700 wonderful issues. Well, turns out I goofed and Papercutz won't be publishing that title. The good news is that we will be publishing a new series called DISNEY GRAPHIC NOVELS and everything I was hoping to feature in WALT DISNEY'S COMICS AND STORIES we'll be able to present in DISNEY GRAPHIC NOVELS! And there's even more good news—WALT DISNEY'S COMICS AND STORIES, as well as UNCLE SCROOGE, DONALD DUCK, and MICKEY MOUSE are all returning to as comicbooks published by our good friends at IDW.

I will admit I was very excited by the thought of editing such a classic comicbook series as WALT DISNEY'S COMICS AND STORIES, but now I'm even more excited to be editing a new graphic novel series that will be featuring the same world-famous and universally beloved cartoon characters. Starting on page 62, we have a special preview of DISNEY GRAPHIC NOVELS #1 "Planes." This still is a dream come true for me, and I sure hope you'll check out this new series. It's the type of comicbook stories that I know will appeal to those who believe in "Faith, trust, and pixie dust"!

Thanks,

Jim

STAY IN TOUCH!

EMAIL: salicrup@papercutz.com
WEB: papercutz.com
TWITTER: @papercutzgn
FACEBOOK: PAPERCUTZGRAPHICNOVELS
REGULAR MAIL: Papercutz, 160 Broadway, Suite 700, East Wing, New York, NY 10038

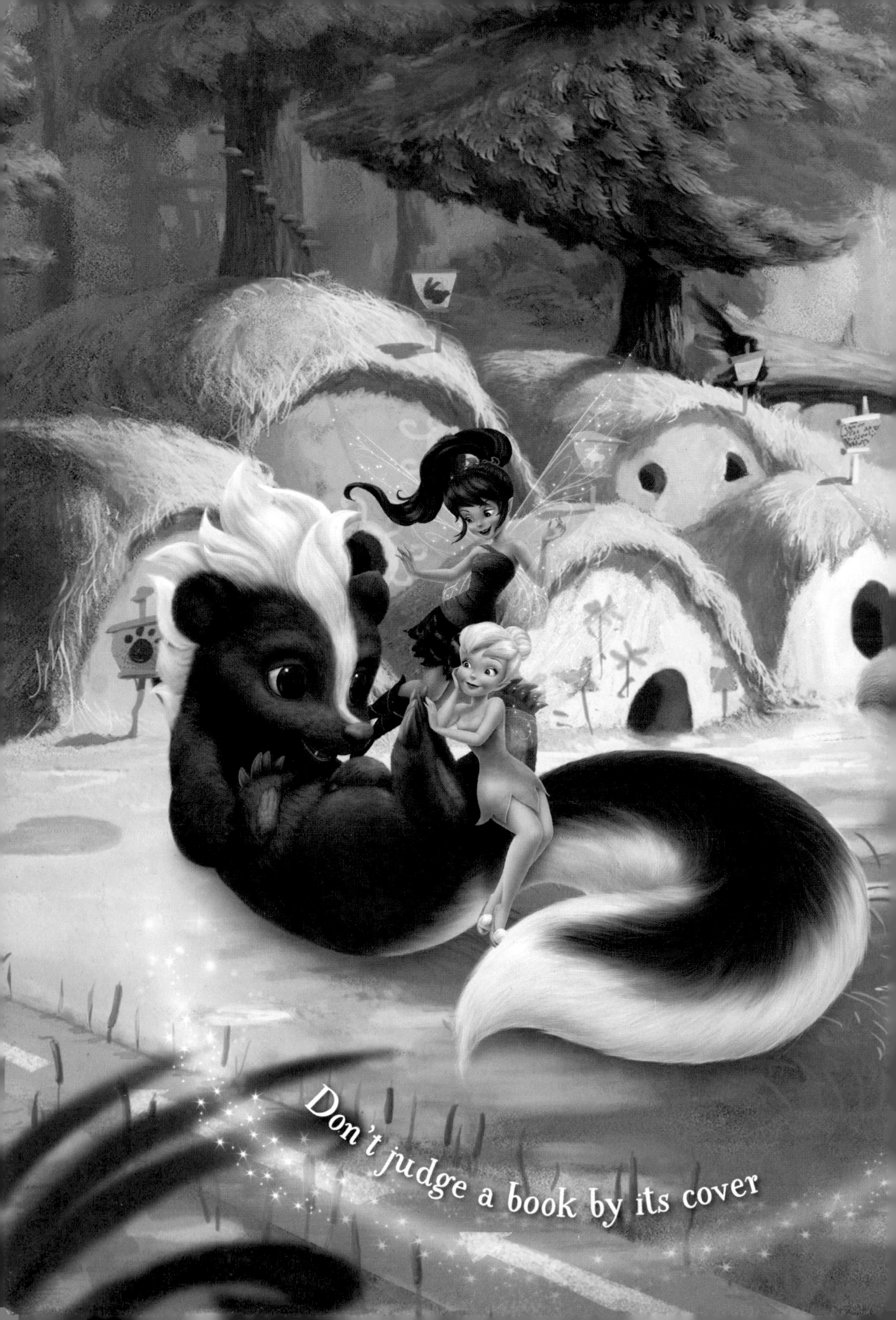
Don't judge a book by its cover

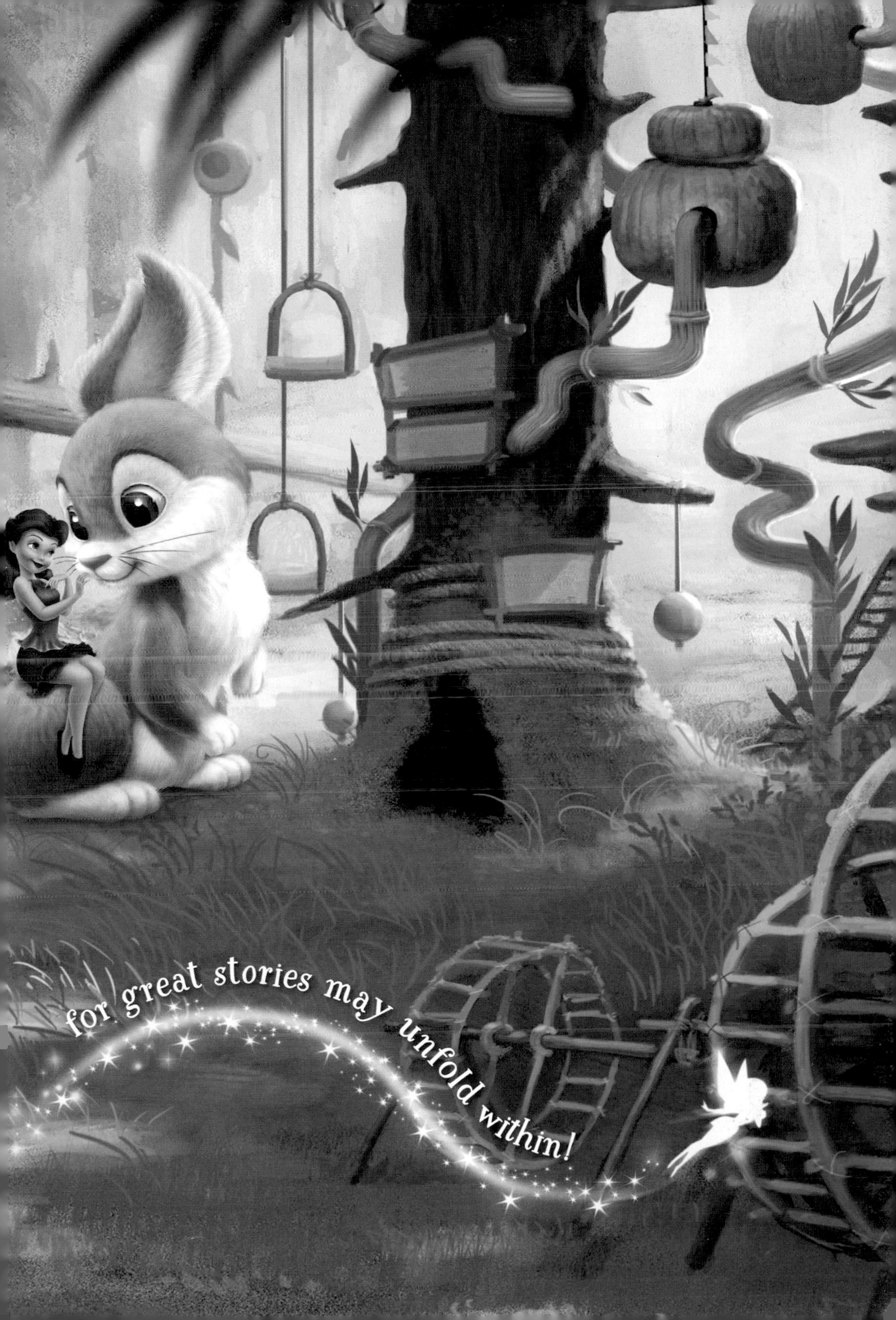
for great stories may unfold within!

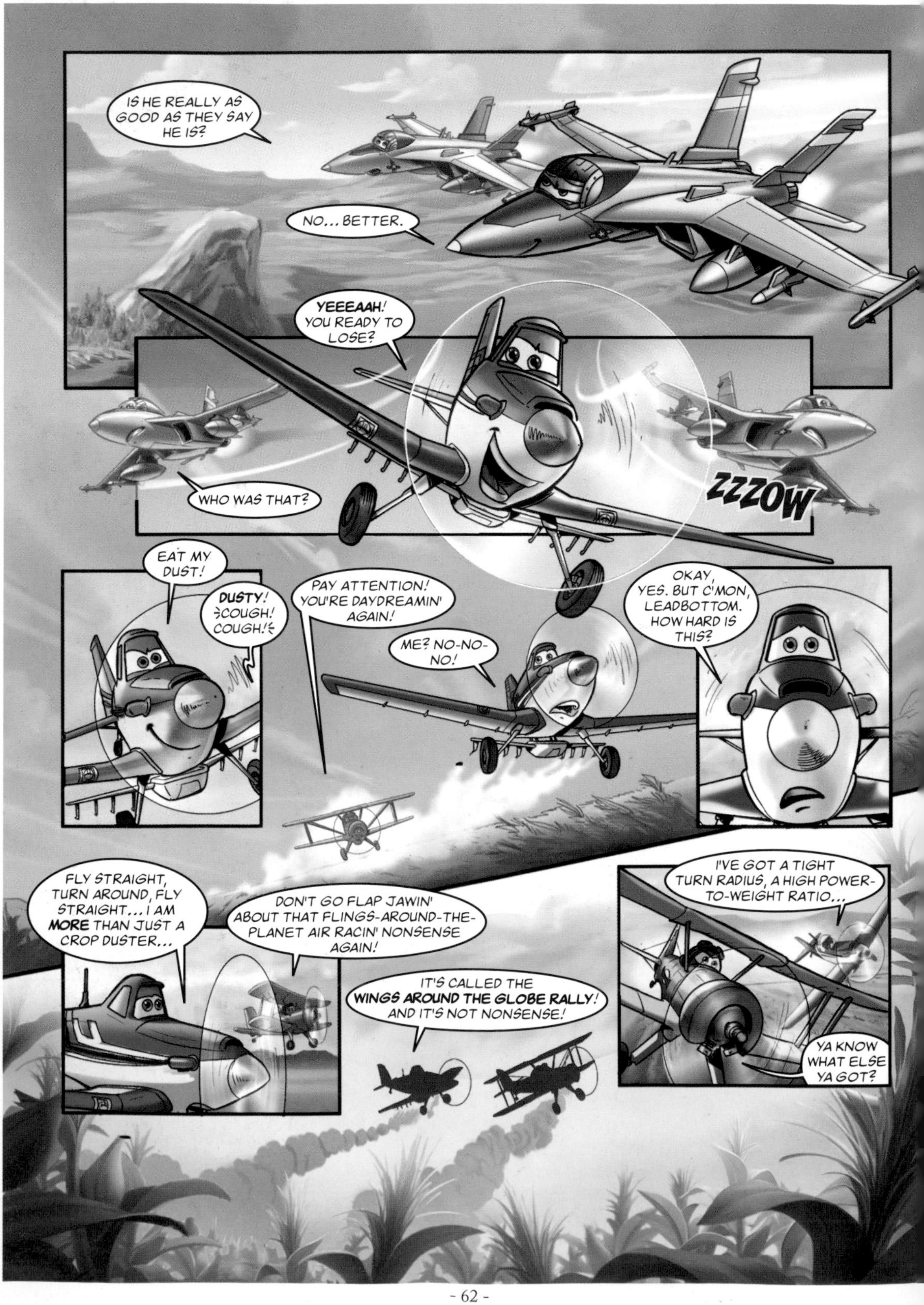
IS HE REALLY AS GOOD AS THEY SAY HE IS?
NO... BETTER.
YEEEAAH! YOU READY TO LOSE?
WHO WAS THAT?
ZZZOW
EAT MY DUST!
DUSTY! COUGH! COUGH!
PAY ATTENTION! YOU'RE DAYDREAMIN' AGAIN!
ME? NO-NO-NO!
OKAY, YES. BUT C'MON, LEADBOTTOM. HOW HARD IS THIS?
FLY STRAIGHT, TURN AROUND, FLY STRAIGHT... I AM MORE THAN JUST A CROP DUSTER...
DON'T GO FLAP JAWIN' ABOUT THAT FLINGS-AROUND-THE-PLANET AIR RACIN' NONSENSE AGAIN!
IT'S CALLED THE WINGS AROUND THE GLOBE RALLY! AND IT'S NOT NONSENSE!
I'VE GOT A TIGHT TURN RADIUS, A HIGH POWER-TO-WEIGHT RATIO...
YA KNOW WHAT ELSE YA GOT?

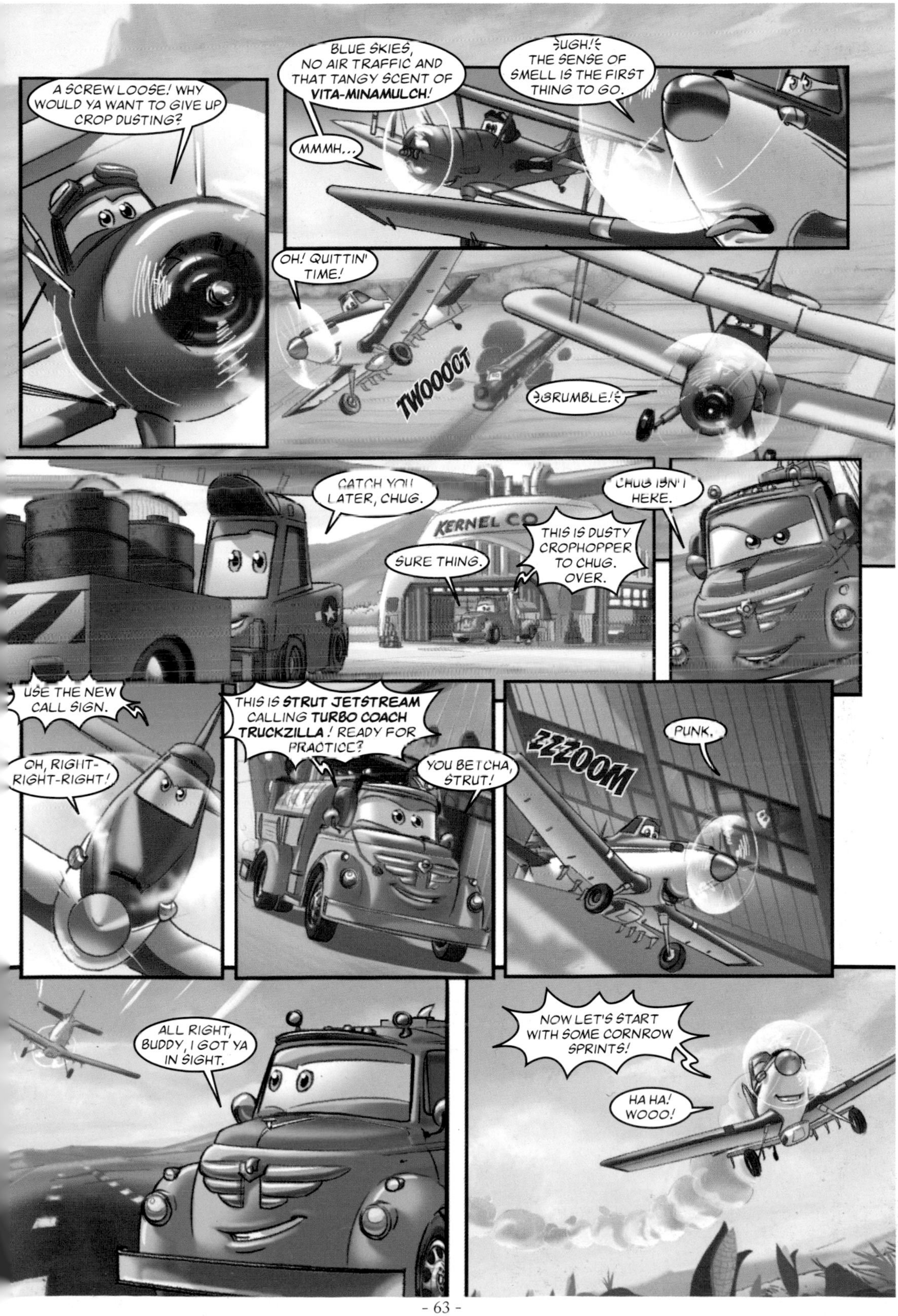
A SCREW LOOSE! WHY WOULD YA WANT TO GIVE UP CROP DUSTING?
BLUE SKIES, NO AIR TRAFFIC AND THAT TANGY SCENT OF VITA-MINAMULCH!
MMMH...
UGH! THE SENSE OF SMELL IS THE FIRST THING TO GO.
OH! QUITTIN' TIME!
TWOOOOT
GRUMBLE!
CATCH YOU LATER, CHUG.
KERNEL CO
SURE THING.
THIS IS DUSTY CROPHOPPER TO CHUG. OVER.
CHUG ISN'T HERE.
USE THE NEW CALL SIGN.
OH, RIGHT-RIGHT-RIGHT!
THIS IS STRUT JETSTREAM CALLING TURBO COACH TRUCKZILLA! READY FOR PRACTICE?
YOU BETCHA, STRUT!
ZZZOOM
PUNK.
ALL RIGHT, BUDDY, I GOT YA IN SIGHT.
NOW LET'S START WITH SOME CORNROW SPRINTS!
HA HA! WOOO!

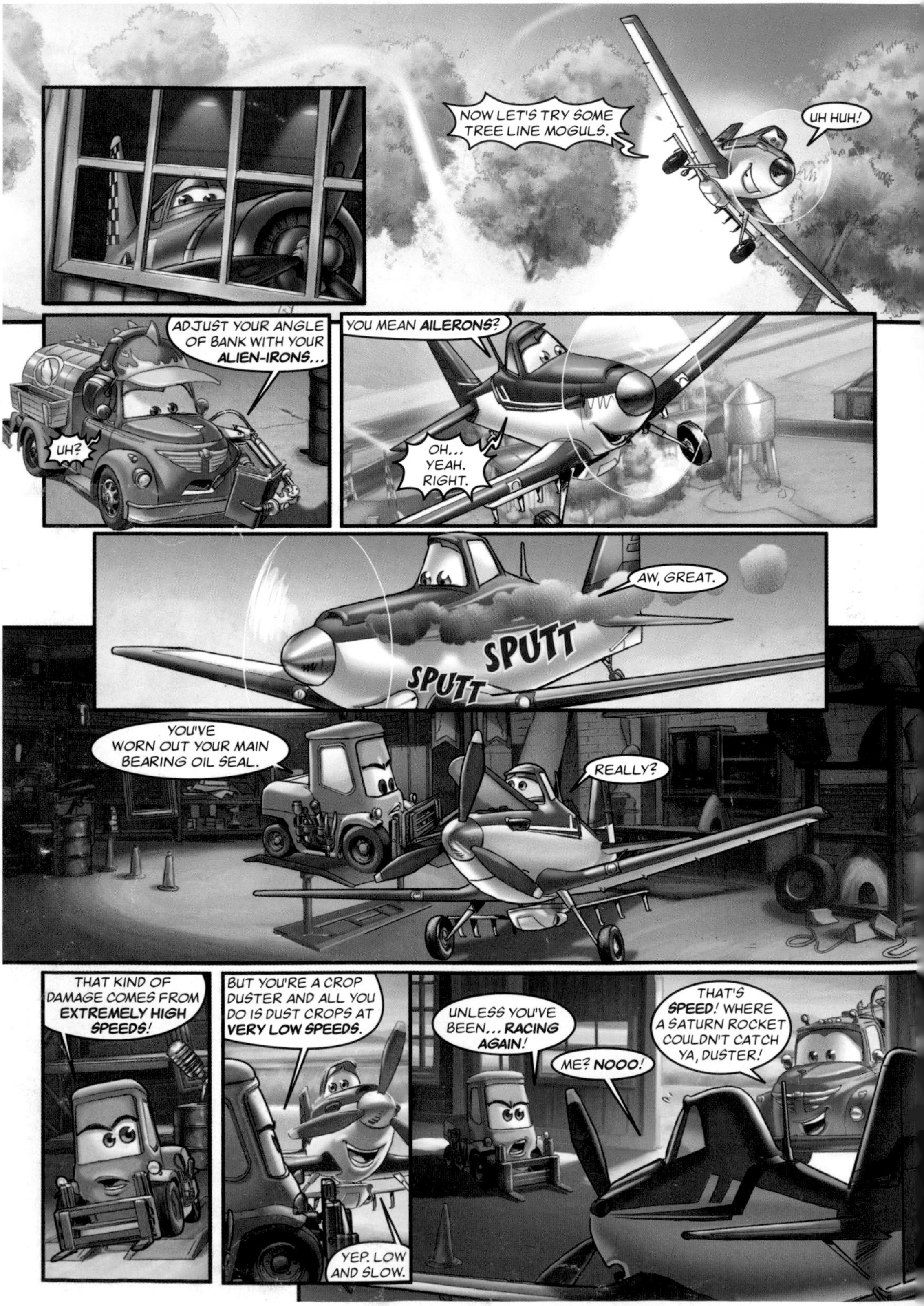
NOW LET'S TRY SOME TREE LINE MOGULS.
UH HUH!
ADJUST YOUR ANGLE OF BANK WITH YOUR ALIEN-IRONS...
UH?
YOU MEAN AILERONS?
OH... YEAH. RIGHT.
AW, GREAT.
SPUTT
SPUTT
YOU'VE WORN OUT YOUR MAIN BEARING OIL SEAL.
REALLY?
THAT KIND OF DAMAGE COMES FROM EXTREMELY HIGH SPEEDS!
BUT YOU'RE A CROP DUSTER AND ALL YOU DO IS DUST CROPS AT VERY LOW SPEEDS.
YEP. LOW AND SLOW.
UNLESS YOU'VE BEEN... RACING AGAIN!
ME? NOOO!
THAT'S SPEED! WHERE A SATURN ROCKET COULDN'T CATCH YA, DUSTER!